www.PlaidforWomen.com

GOOD GIRL GONE PLAID

AMY GALLAGHER

Amy Gallagher © 2013

www.GoodGirlGonePlaid.com
author@amycgal.com

ISBN-10: 0615826024
ISBN-13: 978-06158260-2-8

Published by:

Plaid for Women Publishing
www.PlaidForWomen.com

Edited & formatted for print & eBook by:

Jennifer-Crystal Johnson
www.jennifercrystaljohnson.com

Book cover design by:

Matt Wulff
Fine Art & Illustration
www.mattwulffart.com

To my precious son, Michael Patrick, who brings inspiration to my life daily, and to my husband, Mike, for his faith in God and in me.

Table of Contents

CHAPTER ONE

Nuns are Evil and Boys are Stupid Anyway

The sun is shining. The birds are singing. And the weather is perfect. It's early Saturday morning and my mom is chasing me around the house with a flyswatter. My school is having a carnival and I'm going with my best friend and her boyfriend. I'm only 11 years old, but I thought my mom's reaction was a bit odd. I locked myself in the bathroom, which was a normal course of action given the situation. My heart is pounding as I slam and lock the door shut.

"What boy are you talking about? Do I know him? How do you know him? Riley, open this door immediately!" My mom yelled at the bathroom door while swatting at it with her flyswatter. *Why is she yelling at me and trying to beat me with a flyswatter?* I wondered. *And why is she assuming I plan to do something bad?*

So I yelled back, "It's my BFF, Mary Flaherty, and *her* boyfriend, Andrew Tierney."

I didn't even have a boyfriend. I've never had a boyfriend. I was too afraid to have a real boyfriend. I *wanted* a boyfriend, I thought. I mean, my best friend had a boyfriend. Me personally, I had never truly crushed on a guy before. That is until Shawn Donegal came along. But I was in fifth grade and Shawn was in sixth grade. And he was a real hottie. Except you can't say hottie in a Catholic school, not out loud anyway. Not even in your head either, especially during confession or the priest could smell your lust, one of the Seven Deadly Sins.

You couldn't look a priest in his eyes either because he put up this screen to protect his identity even though we all knew it was Father Flanagan. We could smell his liquored breath. You really can't look into the eyes of a nun, either. People on the outside believe nuns have cross symbols in the middle of their eyes where normal people have a pupil. But that's not true. If

9

anything, nuns have pitch forks... red pitch forks in place of their pupils.

And nuns aren't really women, either. Because if they were real women then I would have many girly girl female mentors who could teach me how to be a girly girl. So being good and a girly girl is tough business. Most of the time, I just stay confused.

There was one nun, though, who was really nice: Sister Abbott, who is now Mrs. Abbott, but that's another story. She dropped her habit for a husband. After she quit her job as a nun, she was actually quite nice, though. She complimented her students with really nice words. She smelled sweet like flowers, and she smiled every day with her pretty pink lipstick.

Mrs. Abbott couldn't teach us every day anymore, though. Since she became a regular person, she could only teach on the "Sisters' Day Out" days. That's when the "lay teachers" like Mrs. Abbott taught us. No one really knows where the nuns go on those days. It is one of the five mysteries of the rosary, I think.

As I was sitting on the bathroom counter, I questioned the whole boy thing. Sometimes I even feel like a boy. I think I'm kind of stuck in the middle, somewhere between a girl and a boy. Just like my name, Riley. One nun told me I have a boy's name and that I should have been blessed with a Catholic girl name like Mary. But my parents probably thought there were already enough Mary girls in Catholic school.

Plus, my parents had so many kids already that naming me Riley would cut down on the confusion in the pick-up line after school so they wouldn't have to weed out all the Mary girls. I feel like it just added to my own confusion. I think I'm more of a tomboy. I like to play sports – soccer, that is. I won the Most Valuable Player trophy last year. I like to play with snakes, too, mainly slimy green garden snakes that slither in between my fingers.

I like to play in creeks and catch crawdads with raw bacon. I use my dad's bacon that he likes to eat on Sunday mornings before mass, but the bacon is usually gone by Sunday. And then Sunday mornings turn from raw bacon to raw rage when my dad yells and cusses like, "*Blankety, blank, blank... where in* the *blank* is my bacon?!" I think my mom knows where the bacon goes, but she doesn't say anything which is pretty cool.

I like to poach frogs, too, and skin fish with the help of Mary's older brother, Johnny, who's a creep except when we're fishing at Mary's grandparents' farm. Mary and I have been friends since kindergarten, and Johnny usually left us alone and hung out with his high school friends.

Some were pretty cute, but way too old. But recently, Johnny seems to follow us around more and more and invites us to do fun things like poaching frogs. Mary said Johnny has a crush on me which I think is completely gross and kinda sick in a way. He's always smiling at me now. Mary's older sister, Dana, says that it's his testosterones going wacky and not a crush. That actually makes me feel better; knowing it might be health-related and he can't help what he does.

I like going over to her grandparents' but their house doesn't have a real bathroom with a shower or bathtub in it. In other words, they don't have running water, which I learned is an under-appreciated resource. So we have to get water from the well to take a bath. I pretend like I'm an actress in a western TV show living in the old Wild West days. I use my imagination like that when I have to wash my hair from a bucket of cold well water. Mary's grandmother said the water is fresh and good for my hair. I wonder if it would make my hair grow long and silky like my older sister's?

I like to play in the tree house that Mary and I built all by ourselves. We found this cool tree in a big field next to the creek behind my house. My dad had some boards in the garage left over from a science project, so we used those to build our tree house. I took his box of nails and his hammer, and the building began. We were gonna live there, but we found out that the field was actually some land that a neighbor owned so, since we built our new tree house in somebody else's tree in somebody else's yard, it didn't last very long.

When Mary comes over to my house, we especially like to sneak off to the underground world of pipes. We wander through these huge people-sized pipes that start at the creek and lead under the ground, under the streets through my neighborhood.

Once we saw a big, black, ugly, hairy spider on the roof of one of the underground pipes. We were scared but we just walked right underneath it. We were on a mission to get to the other street, like underground missionaries. We thought it was cool knowing that we were actually walking underneath all of the neighbors' houses... and big, black, hairy spiders.

My "older" sister, Katherine, never likes to go with me because she is more of a girly girl. I say "older" because technically she is older than me but she doesn't act older and causes trouble all the time, even more than me. She spends all of her time on the phone talking to boys, which my mom says, "only leads to trouble." And ever since Katherine got caught by Sister Peg Leg kissing Shawn in the school library, my mom has been on an anti-boy campaign, which is making *my* life miserable.

Katherine is actually Kat, as she likes to be called, who does bad things that I get in trouble for. That's the joy of being number two. I'm sort of the "fall guy." Except I'm really more of a fallen girl thanks to Kat. That is, by the way, the perfect nickname for her, since Kat has luxuriously long fingernails, like sharp cat claws used to scratch me when we fight. Cats are also sneaky and always land on their feet.

Kat has a cat named Shelby, but my dad said she had to find it a new home because it was just another mouth to feed. One day he kicked Shelby across the living room like a football. He may have been drunk. She didn't land on her feet, though. My dad found a guy who would take Shelby, but that didn't work out so well because when he came to get her, he had a pack of dogs in the backseat of his car and tried to put Shelby in the trunk.

Kat saw the whole thing from the kitchen window and got so steaming mad that she stormed out the front door with her fists clenched, headed straight for dog man's car, and snatched Shelby right out of the guy's trunk before he could slam it shut. Kat marched right back into our house, holding Shelby with her head held high. She looked my dad straight in the eyes for what seemed like a year and then started skipping to her room. I was so afraid for Kat, but my dad just stood there and didn't say a word. I couldn't believe it. Sometimes I think Kat is cool, but I would never tell her that because most of the time she does bad things and then blames me. I already have a list of things I get in trouble for. I don't need Kat adding to my list of sins.

I've learned that it's very difficult to be considered "good" when you're Catholic. Very few Catholics have been blessed with that description. Sister Peg was excellent at pegging the bad, in particular the bad girls. Kat nicknamed her Sister Peg Leg because she had polio as a little girl and wears a fake leg. Me personally, I think it's a bit mean. But *she's* mean, so I guess that evens it out.

Kat has a way of getting all the guys, which is deeply disturbing to me. Of all the boys in the school, it would be my good fortune to crush on Shawn, a sixth grader who has a crush on – who else? – Kat. Shawn is a year older than me and a year younger than Kat. Kat is an eighth grader in the middle school and thinks she's better than those of us in the lower grades. She probably is, but she doesn't have to advertise it.

It doesn't seem fair. When you're one in five kids like I am, you learn a few important lessons at a very early age – especially if you're on the older end of the birth order.

You quickly learn the world doesn't revolve around you. You also learn that if this "economic unit," (a loving term my father uses often) is going to get anything done, you have to cooperate, compromise, and communicate. But you can only communicate to adults when you've been spoken to and only if they ask you a question first. So most of the time, it's better not to speak at all. That's why I write.

So, here I am trying to communicate with my mom through a bathroom door. In the meantime, my brother gets in on the action.

"Riley has a boyfriend, Riley has a boyfriend!" chanted my little brother, Danny.

I quickly opened the door and yelled as he danced around the room in his Superman pajamas.

"Shut up, you stupid ignoramus!" I fired at my brother with anger in my eyes. "You're super stupid, not Superman, by the way."

As I threw in that last jab, my mom rolled her eyes. And I thought to myself, *She's too old to roll her eyes.... I hope she doesn't hit me with that nasty flyswatter.*

Plus, that's the good flyswatter that I use to build my own economic unit. My dad said he would pay me a dime for each fly I swat. He used to pay me a nickel, but I told him I learned about the COLA at school in my economics class. It's the cost of living adjustment. I told my dad that my fly killing business had raised its prices to meet the COLA. I think my dad was so impressed and probably stunned that he agreed.

I'm actually supposed to pick up the dead flies after I steal their last flight, but I think it's way too gross and my dad doesn't pay me enough to do that. And it would make much more sense if my dad made my stupid brother shut the door when he goes outside.

But I make some money so it's helping me build my own personal wealth so I can buy Wacky Wafers and pickle juice and Hot Tamales at the skating rink. But I only indulge during Lent on the "down low" because me and my sibs have to give up candy for Lent. We have this understanding not to tattle on each other. My parents never find out but become suspicious when my mom takes me to the dentist and he says I have cavities. This adds to my parents' confusion which, in the big scheme of things, I think is fair and square.

Right now, though, I hate my brother and my sister, and sometimes I hate my mother, and I really don't like nuns, either. But I can't do anything about any of it. And I'm not even supposed to say the word "hate" because the nuns said it is evil to hate. But I reminded Sister Mary McLary that Jesus said the word hate in the book of Isaiah. And she looked at me with hate in her eyes.

So I finally decided that all I can do is hold out for hope for my baby brother, Ryan. He's a newborn so he's not stupid or evil yet. Why do boys turn stupid as they get older? (That's the question of the universe for sure!) Why are nuns nice to parents but mean and evil to kids, especially when Father Flanagan says it's time to raise the tuition? Why does my mom chase me around the house with a flyswatter? Why do I get blamed for the bad things my sister does?

All I know is that life isn't fair and there are more questions than answers in this world.

CHAPTER TWO

Trouble Followed Me Around Like a Dog

I am experiencing a complete emotional meltdown inside of my body, and nobody in my family seems to notice or even care.

One thing that makes me mad about being in an oversized Catholic family is that no one talks about their feelings in a calm and loving way. My dad yells and belches between gulps of beer. My mom yells, too. She also rolls her eyes when she doesn't believe you, and then sleeps for endless hours. My sisters scream and throw things like bowls of chocolate ice cream, and Kat uses her fancy fingernails to claw ditches in my arms. To some, it probably looks like I'm a cutter, adding even more to my endless list of sins.

I forgot to mention that I have another sister. Her name is Theresa and some people call her Terri for short, but I call her "Terri-ble" and she's ten years old, I think. She's in the fourth grade, so however old that makes her. She's mean like Kat, but not *as* mean because she's younger so I can still be meaner because I am older, after all.

But – and it's a BIG but – Kat and Theresa are tight. They do things together and don't invite me. They tell each other secrets and don't include me. My mom doesn't seem to care, and of course, my dad doesn't seem to notice. It really hurts my feelings, but I don't tell them or my mom. I just try to get them to like me sometimes, but it's really, really hard.

Theresa can be a little back-stabbing and very two-faced. Well, not really a little. Actually, it's more like a lot. Like the other day at recess, she told everyone, and I mean *everyone*, that I still suck my thumb. I used to suck my thumb until I was ten years old, but I don't anymore. I don't really know why I sucked my thumb for so long. So all the kids at recess, even the kids in Theresa's grade, bullied me at recess saying, "Riley sucks her thumb... Riley sucks her thumb...."

I was mortified. Kat used that word one time and I didn't know what it meant, but I'm pretty sure it was because I embarrassed her about something. I can't remember what it was though. But mortified fit my situation at recess. I was so embarrassed. And I wanted to kill my little sister. But I did something even better. I told everyone that Theresa still wets the bed, which she does. That shut her up and I got everyone off my case.

I'm not much of a yeller, but when I got home, I yelled and screamed at Theresa like Mary's sister, Dana, did at me when she took us to a horror movie at the drive-in theater when we were five years old. She said she just needed someone to go with her because she didn't want to go alone and just got her license and some beat up old car that she obviously loved because I spilled my Slurpee and she yelled at me through most of the movie.

"Why, why, why did you tell everyone at school that I still suck my thumb?!" I screamed at Theresa through clenched teeth. "Why do you hate me so much?! What did I ever do to you, anyway?!"

And then I did something that surprised even me; I kicked my bratty little evil sister in the leg and she fell, and of course, started bawling like a baby.

Unfortunately it was one of many days when my mom was asleep because of being sad all the time, and my yelling and Theresa's bawling woke her up. All she heard was my stupid sister crying and so I got in trouble even though I told her what her sweet little St. Theresa did at school.

"Well, Riley, you *don't* suck your thumb anymore. God knows the truth about that and so do you, so there was no harm done," my mom reasoned. "Plus, you're the older sister. You're bigger and you kicked her which is completely unacceptable behavior and you know better. You have to set an example for your younger siblings to be responsible, self-controlled, and forgiving."

I'm thinking to myself, *Excuse me, did she say the word, "forgiving?"*

I don't get this. I mean I understand the whole point of forgiving someone, even someone stupid and evil like Theresa. But I'm a tad confused about why my mom doesn't tell Kat to

16

"forgive" me and for Kat to "set an example." I wish there was an 800-number I could call with questions like this.

But there's not so I spit the truth out like it was Pappaw's chewing tobacco which he spatters in a coffee can even at the supper table.

"This younger creature of yours humiliated me in front of the entire school *and* obviously lied which is a sin, so 'it' needs to apologize," I counseled my mother as though we were in a court of law.

And then my mom said, "Did any of the nuns see any of this or hear your sister tell everyone you sucked your thumb?"

"I don't know. What difference does that make anyway?" I quipped. "Why don't you just believe me?"

And then it occurred to me. My mom was more concerned about what the nuns would think about the Patton family secrets and my mom's "mothering skills." Not only that, but my mom obviously likes St. Theresa more which I already suspected, but that became very clear to me now and made me feel even worse. I realized the damage was done. There was nothing, absolutely *nothing* I could do but scream and yell on the inside until I felt like my stomach was beginning to split open.

And as an afterthought, possibly a twinge of Catholic guilt, my mom said, "Theresa, you need to apologize to your sister."

Terri-ble looked at me like only a self-righteous mutant can, and whispered ever so softly, "Sorry."

So I said, "Yeah, you are sorry," and stormed off in the direction of the broken sliding glass patio door. I had kicked in the glass and shattered it the other day when my stupid brother refused to unlock it and let me in when it started raining outside. My soccer skills come in handy sometimes… except when I break glass doors.

"Riley, you come back here young lady," my mom said in the stern voice she thinks she has, but she's really just weak and mean.

I yelled, "Whatever!"

So now I guess I'm a yeller, too. I hate that.

The only person in my family who doesn't yell is little Ryan. But he does cry a lot, very loud actually, and that does get on my last nerve. And I really don't like putting his pacifier in his mouth because it's usually on the floor with the dead flies. But I have to admit, sometimes it's OK because it shuts him up.

My goal in life is to be out of this house as much as I possibly can while going to school and without getting in trouble with my parents, and the law, or in my case, the nuns at my school. So I head to the backyard toward the creek where I sit on my favorite rock to watch the tadpoles speed through the water like the sperm we saw on a sex education film at school last year. It's just gross to even think about, but it helps me think of boys like tadpoles and then they grow up to be frogs.

I guess that's why there's that story about the princess kissing the frog and it turns into the handsome prince and they live happily ever after. I always wondered why a girl, especially a really pretty girl, would have to kiss a frog just to get a prince.

That's messed up. I think I will rewrite all of those stupid fairy tales when I grow up.

As I sit and mull over the wretched family I have to live with temporarily, my mind drifts toward the next day at school where I know in advance that I'm going to get in trouble about something.

Trouble. We actually have a dog named Trouble. He's a mutt, but he's a very cute mutt and doesn't dig holes in the backyard or eat my mom's shoes. He poops in the house sometimes, but so does my bunny, Herbie; except you can't see Herbie's poopy balls because they are so tiny and hide between the two-inch high green and blue shag carpet that Pappaw and Uncle Stephen put in.

At that moment, I figured out why we named our dog Trouble. It's because that's the word that is plastered on the walls in every room in my house... T-R-O-U-B-L-E.

"You're gonna get in trouble," ... "You're nothing but trouble," ... "I'm in trouble again," ... "Don't tell mom and dad or else I'll say it's your fault and you'll get in trouble."

A few years ago, our dog Trouble ran away. Honestly, I really couldn't blame him. Poor dog. Smart dog. I only wish he had asked me to come along with him. It was a very sad time.

Interestingly, though, it was also a time when our entire family was sad about the same thing at the same time and we

18

actually talked about our sad feelings. Silence and solitude, if for a split second of time, graced our home. It was eerie and beautiful, and I don't use that word very often.

Actually, I've never used it to describe my family.

It was strange and familiar at the same time. It felt good though. Like there was a war going on, and everyone in my family was in the same platoon and we were working together without trying to kill each other. Instead, we were coming together as one to serve on the most important mission of our lives. We were going to find our lost dog.

And then out of thin air, my dad came home one day after work and said he received a call from a lady who said she thinks she may have found our dog. It was a miracle from Heaven as Sister Maria says when she gets a day off. We were all so excited and happy all at the same time. For that moment in time, nobody was fighting or yelling in my house.

As it turned out, Trouble was in another city at a lady's house that my dad worked with. At that point, I began to smell trouble.

Later, we discovered that my dad had given Trouble to his co-worker to save money on groceries. Or as he puts it, to rid himself of one more mouth to feed. But when my dad realized all of his children were devastated for days, I guess his pickled brain triggered sort of a guilt response.

Guilt actually looked good on my dad.

He looked like a man at peace and was willing to surrender. We realized that my dad, or rather my dad's drinking, was the enemy our platoon was fighting all along. And then suddenly, my mom took on this position of power in our house. Yet, she didn't need to say a word. She just gave my dad this look. Kind of like the evil nuns at school do with their pitch fork eyes.

Kat said she heard mom telling dad he was now the one in trouble and will be sleeping in the dog house. Trouble didn't even have a dog house so I'm not really sure what she meant by that. But I knew it wasn't good.

As it turned out, trouble seemed to have found my dad versus the other way around. For some reason, it felt kinda good to know my dad was the one in trouble for once. He seemed to be a little nicer to all of us, too. I think my mom cut off his beer supply.

I wish my dad would get in trouble more often.

Nuns have this supernatural power to triple the size of trouble in a nanosecond. What seems like an innocent mistake to a normal person mysteriously transforms into a broken commandment. And suddenly, without even a minute to form your excuse, you find yourself with your head down walking a death march to the closest confessional.

I might be a lawyer when I grow up because I believe some people, especially children, are innocent. I would make tougher nun laws my first priority.

I would really like to take the flyswatter permanently away from my mom's hand and sit her down at the kitchen table. I would like to share a glass of Kool-Aid, or even a really tall glass of chocolate milk, and tell her that my feelings are hurt when she assumes I'm going to do something bad, like go to the carnival to make out with a boy.

I want to tell her that I don't do those things, and remind her that Kat does those things. I want to tell her that I am Riley, not Kat. I want to tell her that I am smart enough to know that there are more important things in this world besides boys. Although I don't know what, but there's got to be something more important.

I want to tell my mom that she hurts my feelings when she always takes Theresa's side just because she's younger than me, especially when Theresa does or says something bad. I just want to share my feelings with my mom, but I don't really know how to describe what I feel about all of this. I think I feel sad, but then I get so mad like my ears are going to pop off my head because the steam inside is so hot. And then it goes to complete and chaotic confusion when I don't understand why my mom doesn't take my side for once.

And then I remember. I am a number. I am one in five. Actually, I'm one in eight if you consider my mom and dad and Trouble.

When you're in a big family, your feelings really don't matter that much. In fact, you can check you selfishness at the curb, thank you very much, because there are more important things that need attention, and you're not one of them.

So I write my feelings in my Plaid Sad/Mad/Glad Father God and Mother Mary journal that I keep hidden in a shoe box under my bed with my Girl Scout flashlight. It comes in handy on nights when I can't sleep, especially when I'm sad or mad.

"Look, Mom. I don't have a boyfriend. It's just a carnival. Nothing bad is going to happen. I'm meeting Mary. You know, my best friend Mary Flaherty?" I try to reassure my mom that I will not run away and get married.

I will not smoke cigarettes or do drugs behind the portables like the freaks do. I won't make out or drink. Worst case scenario is that I might have fun just being a normal soon-to-be teenage girl who wants to get some cotton candy and a big doughy pretzel with some mustard to dip it in, and the biggest Dr. Pepper I can find.

We'll have to use Mary's money because I don't have any and Mary's parents are loaded, anyway. She even has her own horse, which is way cool. I want a horse so badly, but my parents don't want anything else they have to feed which didn't make any sense to me because horses eat grass which is free. And apples and carrots, but I was willing to use my flyswatter money to help pay for those, or possibly even grow my own garden.

So I decided to collect rocking horses and carousels instead until I get older when I will run and be free on a ranch with nothing but horses.

My mom looks at me with skepticism. I wish she could learn to trust me. I am not a bad girl like Kat. I may do silly, stupid stuff once in a while because I'm still a kid. But I am actually more responsible than her oldest.

"Well, alright, then." The words slowly dribbled out of my mom's mouth. "But your father's science fair is tonight so I have to help him get everything together."

Ah, relief in sight. I can smell freedom from the gut-speckled flyswatter.

"So, Kat, I need you to take Riley and your brother to the carnival." As my mom swift kicked this last jab, my heart fell through my stomach to the floor with a heavy thud.

Great, I thought to myself. *This is not my life.*

"Y'all need to be home from the carnival by 4 o'clock to bless your science fair project," my mom softly instructed.

"You mean ask dad what experiment he put my name on?" I asked sarcastically.

My dad, the great scientist, is the president of our city's annual science fair. He was a physics major and was very… well, scientific. I always thought he and my mom made an odd pair. Like they shouldn't have happened. But then they wouldn't have created five science fair projects like us kids. Their parenting mishaps are like science experiments gone awry.

At last year's exhibit, I won a blue ribbon for proving a rock could float. Pumice floats. Who knew? Better yet, who cared? It was my dad's brainstorm, as were all of the other winning exhibits that were entered on behalf of the Patton family. He's just mad. Mad as in the scientist kind of mad, like crazy. But he's the other kind of mad, too, especially when he's drinking. He's both kinds of mad.

Most of our nuns are mad, too. Sister Matilda Madigan, or, "Sister Mad," which more aptly describes her holy meanness, is my homeroom nun. She's one of those 'fire and brimstone' crusaders. She's just plain ole mean.

And I'm not the only kid in school who feels that way. She has this ungodly power that makes you feel like you're gonna burn in hell after one of her lectures. Sometimes she doesn't even have to say anything. She just gives you one of her special "intellectual spankings." The way her eyes beam with red pitchforks in place, and then mysteriously, you feel your face burning and your eyes start to water. It's way freaky and quite scary.

One time, we had a new priest visit our parish. I remember him saying, "Our selfishness can hide God like a cloud can hide a star. But a star still shines and God still loves."

He didn't last very long.

I overheard one of the nuns saying that he was too nice. Nice would have been fine with me. It would be nice to at least have nice at home. It's even worse when you're a big Catholic family because, at least in my house, you're never supposed to take the last of anything, even if you're starving and there's one dinner roll left and you're the only person left at the table because everyone else is finished and full. Sacrifice and starvation or sin. The choice is yours. It's all part of the big Catholic family way of life.

"Come on, y'all. Hurry up," yells Kat like it's her call of duty to order us around as she femininely twirls her long black pony tail.

I'm rushing out of my room after changing clothes fifty times and finally realize that a closet full of Catholic school uniforms and military blouses leaves me no room for cool and creative clothing for weekend wear. So I throw on an old tie-dyed T-shirt with a peace sign on the front that I made at Girl Scout camp and a pair of hand-me-down hip huggers, bell bottoms, or low riders, whatever they're called, from Kat.

"Riley Claire," snaps my mom. "Where is your bra?" While I appreciate that most girls my age should be wearing a bra, it is unnecessary for me. "I don't need a bra, Mom. Remember, I take after dad in that department?"

I figure the peace sign serves as a kind of shield, a breast plate if you will. Then I begin to feel sort of righteous like St. Michael and I suddenly feel empowered for a brief moment in time.

In fact, I think I look pretty cool, unlike at school where I have to wear my blue and red plaid uniform, which is actually a skirt with a bib. When you get to seventh grade, though, you get to get rid of the bib which I really don't understand. That's the time when girls are really starting to grow boobs and wear bigger bras, and bras can look weird and ugly if they don't fit right.

Bras are pointless and wearing one is futile if you don't have anything to put in them. Seems like the nuns would make us wear bibs to cover our woman-ness as we get older. Me, I don't have to worry about boobs, or bras for that matter.

I'm probably a 28AAAAAAAAAAAAAAAAAAAAAA anyway.

I guess that's why I feel like a boy, and because I look like my dad and my brothers instead of my mom and my sisters. I was probably adopted. Once I decided to run away to find my adoptive parents, but it got dark so I went back home. I pretend that my adoptive parents are nice and talk like librarians. They don't yell at kids, don't get drunk or sleep all day, or pick favorites.

I really need to get a life.

I'm thinking about joining the Peace Corps or something far, far away without parents.

While I ponder the thought of my international adventure, I'm off to the carnival shadowed by my sister and silenced by my younger brother. It'll have to do right now. I am getting kind of excited, though. I heard they were gonna have a real fortune teller at the carnival this year, which I always thought was sacrilegious. Someone said that the fortune teller had been a nun for a long time, but got fired by the parish priest. Interesting. I wonder what a nun has to do to get fired by a priest. I already like this lady.

I would much rather be a fortune teller than a nun anyway. I'm even more excited to ask her about her nun life and what she did to get in trouble. Plus, I'm desperate for answers, and would like to hear about a future with lots of rainbows and no flyswatters and absolutely no trouble whatsoever.

Except my dog.

CHAPTER THREE

Thou Shalt Not Love Boys

For some reason, my fifth grade year seemed to revolve around love. More specifically, boys.

At the carnival, I traded my stuffed yellow snake that I won at my dad's science fair with my BFF Mary for a pin she stole from her older sister, DeeDee, which is Dana's nickname. Why do the oldest sisters always get nicknames? It was hard giving up the snake, but I thought the pin was way cooler.

It's a big, round, red, white, and blue pin that screams, "I LOVE BOYS." I decided to wear it to school, but I had to put it on in the bathroom when I got to school so my mom wouldn't see it. I pinned it on the collar of my boring white blouse. It made the blouse prettier, and I thought it was very patriotic. It's an election year and we are studying political campaigns in our U.S. History class. I wanted to bring it like a "show and tell" trinket.

I think Sister Mad either overlooked my patriotic spirit or misunderstood my intentions entirely. I walked into class with a big smile and my big pin, and sat down feeling very proud. Mary looked at me from across the classroom and let out a loud sound kinda like a combination of a laugh and a cough.

I'm not sure what I was thinking, and that was the problem. I wasn't thinking, I was feeling. And feelings can get you into big trouble, especially if you have nuns for teachers and a mother who carries a flyswatter.

Sister Mad pulled me by my ear out of the classroom and into the hallway, then looked at me with her evil eyes and said, "Riley, you are an 11-year-old young lady and a Catholic schoolgirl at that. Good girls don't advertise their love for the opposite sex. It's lust and it's a sin."

OK. That was really weird hearing a nun say the word, "sex." And, uh, was I a young lady or a school girl? Because in my book, you can't be both.

By the time I was born, my parents had been married for almost four years and were parenting their first and only child, Kat, who was two when I was born. In the meantime, however, my mother gave birth to twin boys, Peter and Paul, who were born three months too early… they died because they came too soon.

I think my mom and dad are still sad from it because they never talk about them. And then I came along and I wasn't a boy. I was a girl which translated into huge disappointment. And the older I became, the more I realized that I looked like my father and my sisters looked like my mother. I became interested in sports, unlike my sisters, which fueled the boy profile and tomboy demeanor I inherited.

Kat had long, black, silky, beautiful hair parted down the middle. No bangs. Sleek. Sexy. Sophisticated. I had bangs. Kat was definitely born with more princess DNA than me. I had long straight hair too, but I got it cut into a short bob the summer before I started fifth grade. Although I probably had the makings of a princess, I was rather clumsy. I can't walk, talk, and chew gum at the same time like Kat and her girly girl friends can. The nuns won't let us chew gum in uniform anyway.

Bruises lined my legs from ankle to thigh, mainly from doing stupid boy stunts like jumping from the tallest tree in the neighborhood. One time I took the chain off my bike and rode it down the steepest hill after a good rain. The roads were nice and slick which made it easier to crash into the neighbor's yard at the bottom of the hill. One of my mom's friends thought I was suicidal.

To make matters worse, my parents gave me a boy's name. No other girl in my entire school is named Riley. The only other weird girl name in school is Shawn's sister, Irene. My mom says I'll be glad about my special name when I get older and compete in the business world. Yeah, right – if I live that long. Most of the time I feel like an oddball desperate to fit in. But where? Besides that, I don't belong in the business world. I'm joining the Peace Corps in a land far, far away.

When we finally got to the carnival, I worked up a smooth line to convince my sister that Danny is the only kid here who needs a babysitter. But then I spotted him. Short, brown, sort of wavy hair with dark brown eyes and shiny white teeth framed by those kissable lips. He smiled. His eyes twinkled and I melted like ice cream on a hot summer afternoon.

Shawn. I knew he was looking at me with the excitement of a sailor returning from sea to smooch his girl. I inhaled deeply with a sigh so loud that I began to blush and feel like my face was sunburned by a million suns.

My stomach churned around and around like a clothes dryer filled with dancing butterflies.

"Hi, Kat," he said.

OK, I'm invisible. I pinched my arm to make sure that I could still feel. *Yup. I'm still alive on this planet. Too bad Shawn doesn't notice me.*

And before I could turn my head to face him, Kat said, "Here Riley, take Danny for a ride." And they were gone. In an instant, a flash, such a short span of time; even my quick-minded self was stumped. I had been dumped, by the love of my life and my evil sister.

And then I saw Mary and her boyfriend, Andrew, off in the distance laughing and sharing a windblown swirl of pink cotton candy. I was really feeling even more invisible now. So much for going to the carnival with my best friend. I felt like I just got a second dumping. Now I was feeling like a good flyswatter beating might have been less painful.

CHAPTER FOUR

Doomed and Dumped, but Not Discouraged

Then, I see Irene.

"Hey Irene," I notice quickly that she, too, has a younger brother in tow. To make matters worse, her brother Jimmy has a crush on me. One day at school, I found a note inside my desk. It read, "I love you Riley, Love, Jimmy." Great. A second grader has a crush on me. Crushes can be very messy at times, and very inconvenient.

"Why don't you kids go play on the moon jump together?" grinned Irene. *She's so smart*, I thought to myself. Send these pesky, bratty brothers to the moon. What was the harm, a first grader and a second grader together at a school carnival guarded by nuns? Good thinking, Irene.

The carnival grounds were littered with tents and tables filled with games, cake walks, pretzel stands, hot dogs, cotton candy, and everything sinful you could imagine. It's weird watching a nun eat a hot dog. I didn't think they could eat that stuff, at least in public anyway.

I have to say that Irene is probably the coolest friend I have. She's not my BFF, though, because she will have to move in a year or so. But she's new and wildly different. She's even been to a public school before, which is highly respected by private school girls... not by the nuns, though. Her dad is in the military and they live on the Air Force base where they have their own movie theater with really cheap nachos that I spilled all over a man once when I tried getting back to my seat in the dark.

I like Irene. Irene's cool. The Donegal family has traveled all over the world. Irene is the only girl in school who refused to wear the prescribed saddle oxfords. She has a sense of style I can't explain. And instead of oxfords, she wears clogs. Not the normal clogs, but clogs from a foreign country called Holland. They make clickety sounds when she walks. And she's real little so the clicketies are like petite baby clicks scurrying down the hall.

Irene also wears these cute and tiny earrings that match her cute and tiny ears. She's sort of a princess in a cool sort of way, unlike Kat who is an evil witch princess. Irene is the only girl I know who is both a tomboy *and* a princess. Some days Irene even comes to school with shiny lips.

The nuns have reported Irene's list of school dress code sins to her parents and issued Irene a behavior card. But her mother ignored the warning. I don't think they're really Catholic, either. They just have a lot of kids. And they pay enough tuition and donation money at Sunday mass to keep Father Flanagan happy, which is very hard to do especially when he hasn't had any of his "Jesus juice" which is really the holy wine in disguise.

Irene is like my hero friend even though she can be a princess at times. But she's a nice princess. Irene's also a "base kid" which is a kid who lives on the local Air Force base. The school has a good deal of base kids that come and go like my dad's beer. The nuns said it's OK for base kids to attend school at St. Paul's. I'm beginning to realize that the nuns make all the rules... not the Pope or Father Flanagan.

I overheard Sister Nehib call them "Army brats" before, which I think is very rude, but then again we secretly nicknamed Sister Nehib, Sister "Body Parts" because her name sounds like knee-hip. My mom said we're related to Sister Nehib, but I sure can't see any resemblance. I decided it's best to keep this situation a family secret.

All of the nuns pray that the Brats would become Catholic so that their behavior would improve. But the nuns haven't figured out yet that just because a girl is a Catholic with princess DNA doesn't mean she's gonna be a good Catholic school girl. I mean look at my sister, Kat. Irene is definitely a special student in the eyes of the nuns. I think they may have even added a few rosary beads just for the base kids, especially the ones with parents who break the dress code commandments.

For some reason, the nuns kinda respect those parents more. Nuns are very confused people, and very difficult to understand.

Catholic school is so complicated.

The only thing about making friends with a base kid is that they move right after you become close friends. Base kids, like Irene, come in and out of St. Paul's. The Mary's are the only ones who stay every school year, and they get boring after a while.

Irene is like a whimsical Irish fairy. She smiles all the time. She has blue eyes, long light brown wavy hair, long black eyelashes, and lots of freckles. She has dimples on both sides of her smile that work like bookends to hold her smile in place all day. I think most of the nuns hate everything about Irene, which is probably the reason I like her so much. The nuns even hate her smile. But they know her dad will be relocated in a few short weeks or months, so they don't waste their evil energy on short-timers. Plus, Irene's family has lots of kids which means a big, fat stack of tuition money.

"I wish I had petite ballerina feet like you and could wear your clogs," I said with a twinge of envy. Her dainty feet were protected by the wooden footwear that added confidence to her walk. My feet were huge like puppy feet which creates a goofy, clumsy gait like an overworked Irish draught horse.

"I saw your sister with my brother," she said softly. She slowly spoke the words as though to ease the pain. "He wasn't holding her hand, though." *She is such a good friend,* I thought to myself.

"I know. Let's get our fortune told." Her smile broke through her dimples as she grabbed my hand and clicked off to the tent where the genie-like lady wearing a chiffon veil was hiding her lower face along with our futures.

The fortune teller's eyes were thickly lined with purple eyeliner. Blue eye shadow caked her lids and heavy black mascara created spooky spider leg lashes. How she got past the nuns in that costume was indeed a mystery only to be revealed by her crystal ball and tarot cards.

As we sat down at the fortune teller's table, the veiled mystery lady took my arm and turned my hand over with my palm facing up. She started to massage my hand a little, which tickled so I laughed.

Then she squeezed my hand like a comforting hug. I started to relax and heave a greatly needed sigh.

Breathe, I said to myself. We got rid of our little brothers. I have to say that I was relieved to be relieved of my babysitting duties for the moment. It felt good to be "off work" for once and just play like a real life kid.

"I see, I see," the lady whispered with confidence.

"What do you see? I can't see anything," I said to her as she stroked my palm.

"You will have a very busy life," she spoke ever so deeply and very slow.

"That's nothing new. I could have told you that," I retorted.

"Hush, child," she immediately spiked her tone of voice with an air of authoritative meanness. For a moment, I thought she was a nun. And then I remembered she was a nun in a former life, probably a really mean one. Just my luck.

And then she proceeded with more of a death wish than a promising future.

"You will have three children," she said with surety. It wasn't the kind of fortune I was expecting. Irene giggled. And then as an afterthought, she added, "Or you will be married three times."

I felt like a bowling ball just shot through my heart on its way down the lane of losers.

"What! What kind of fortune teller tells that to a kid at a school carnival? I'm only in fifth grade! Come on, Irene, let's get outta here. This lady is mean and depressing, and still has nun blood in her."

You can take the fortune teller out of the nun, but you can't take the nun out of the fortune teller. Talk about feeling doomed.

Doomed and dumped all on the same day.

Years of Catholic schooling combined with a future of untold horror. I was better off not getting my fortune told. Now I understand why the nuns say fortune telling is sacrilegious; maybe nuns are right about some things. I'm struggling to understand, though, why the nuns even allowed Former-Nun-Turned-Fortune-Teller into the carnival in the first place.

With a fortune like mine, I slowly sank into a serious depression beyond my own recognition. I think the school should fire that fortune teller. She's a *mis*-fortune teller, and a liar at that.

I want to tell on her, but I'm not a tattle-teller like Theresa. Plus I like the fact that the fortune teller got fired from her nun job. That was kinda cool. Sounds like she kicked the habit and became some kind of gypsy-hippie-rebel-warrior woman.

I'm still holding on to hope, though. I'm more of a hope-a-holic than a romantic. I'm secretly longing for gypsy woman to tell me that Shawn is going to fall madly in love with me, and Kat's face would break out with a bunch of zits real soon. I guess I could pray about it. Sister Marie Salvador said that when you ask God for something, he will answer your prayers.

I'll give it a try. What do I have to lose, anyway? I crawl under my bed to grab my God box and my Mad/Sad/Glad Father God and Mother Mary journal, and I begin to write out what I want and then pray aloud; but not too loud.

"Oh God, please put gigantic and terribly gross zits on my sister's face. Thank you, God. I love you so much. And one more thing, if you decide to put zits on her face, then I promise not to be bad or get in trouble for the rest of my life."

I'm feeling pretty good about my life now. Note to self: former nuns are lousy fortune tellers.

CHAPTER FIVE

Picking Friends is Tricky Business

Monday morning brought more drama to our school.

Mary, Irene, and I overheard a parent complaining to Sister Mad about the mis-fortune teller. As it turns out, she had an affair with Father Flanagan which means she broke the 4th commandment, Thou Shall Not Commit Adultery. And that's the reason she had to trade her rosary beads and prayer cards in for a crystal ball and tarot cards.

Our homeroom nun made us put a white envelope for our parents in our backpacks. Something tells me we'll be getting a new priest very soon. I didn't have to have a crystal ball to know that.

Apparently this particular parent actually *saw* Father Flanagan and the Mis-Fortune Teller talking "lustfully" behind her carnival tent. I'm not sure what that means, but it sounds like it would qualify as a major gross out. There are minor gross outs, too, but this situation is not one of them. It's probably an actual sin.

"I think that is disgustingly gross," I said to Irene.

"I know. I almost threw up my Twinkie," she replied which made me laugh. "I kinda hope she gets in trouble with the Pope."

"But she can't because she's not a nun anymore," I reasoned.

"Maybe Father Flanagan will get in trouble," giggled Irene.

"Not a chance," I said. "Father Flanagan *never* gets in trouble."

"I don't know. He did something really bad this time with that lust thing," explained Irene.

"I wonder what the letter says," I pondered.

"It's probably another letter asking for money," chimed Brian. He's a red-headed, freckle-faced know-it-all. But he's usually right about these things.

"My dad isn't gonna be very happy about that if that's the case," I shared.

"Mine either," said Brian.

But this time the envelope was actually sealed shut with nun spit, which some believe is where holy water comes from. Normally, the money-hungry letters aren't sealed which means we can read the letter before we get home and find out if it's another, "Your child is in trouble.... blah, blah, blah," letter.

"It must be really bad since it's a formally sealed letter," I said to Brian who had this worried look on his face that made some of his freckles connect up, making him look like he had a supernatural, amazingly dark tan on his face.

And I think to myself, *Brian must have done something really bad.* He had that Catholic guilt look.

At the end of the school day, Sister Mad did the announcements like she always does. I think she was selected out of all the nuns because she has this really deep man's voice that sounds more like Frankenstein gargling with gravel.

She said, "Father Flanagan has decided to move to a new church school." Sister Mad made it sound like it was Father's idea, but we all knew the truth. I think the priest is supposed to be the head of the church, but Sister Mad controls all of the tuition money and student punishment. She's *really* good with the latter.

Apparently Father Flanagan suddenly became the new priest at St. Jude's Catholic Church and School, aka the Catholic School of Male Dominion according to Sister Mad. It's the only Catholic school with more priests and monks, and only the really mean and unhappy nuns teach at St. Jude's.

St. Jude is also the Saint of Hopeless Causes, which makes perfect sense considering it's an all-boys' school and probably a perfect place for Father Flanagan. Through her wicked dragon breath, I overheard Sister Mad say he was a hopeless cause. She probably has a crush on him.

He was told he could no longer be friends with the Mis-Fortune Teller or any female adults for that matter. I read the letter after my dad read it since he laid it on the kitchen table for all the world to read, so I didn't feel guilty. If you want to know what's going on in this world, you have to have good detective skills, so you can't let guilt interfere with any information-gathering mission.

After reading the letter, I kinda felt sad for Father Flanagan. Perhaps he could become friends with the mean nuns at St. Jude since they aren't really females. Regardless of gender, though, he obviously never learned how to pick friends. Maybe his parents never taught him. But then again, my parents didn't teach me and I am a highly-skilled friend picker. In fact, I have learned that picking a friend is a highly strategic skill.

For example, if you crush on a guy at school and you know he has a sister, you must become friends with his sister. It works out like a charm when she is in a grade close to yours. If his sister is much younger than you, then hopefully you have a younger sister in her class and you can convince your sister to become best friends with her.

The most important thing about picking a friend is access. Access is key.

Take for example my BFF, Mary. For all my other Mary friends, I have to use last names because all of my friends are named Mary. BFF Mary, Mary O'Donnell and Mary Tierney. St. Paul's Catholic Preparatory School is full of student Mary's.

Many of the nuns are named Mary, too. So at times it gets confusing for the students, but not for the nuns because they grew up with a bunch of Mary's. It's probably a requirement to get into nun school. I don't think it was a requirement to get into St. Paul's, though, because my name's not Mary.

I'm pretty sure the Mary nuns made better grades in nun school. They probably had nicknames, too, like Mary 1, Mary 2, Mary 3, etc. so the head nun could keep track of who's who.

Mother Mary, however, was the greatest Mary of all the Mary's. And there is only one Mother Mary. We pray to her every Friday morning during our weekly mass at school and every Sunday with my family.

St. Paul's is also known as the School for Catholic Higher Orders or "SCHO" for short. Why the nuns and priests and bishops and kings who came up with the name left off the O and the L escapes even my elementary school brain. I mean it's a

S-C-H-O-O-L! I don't understand their thinking and why they can't spell.

I also don't understand that whole Catholic guilt thing.

One night, I heard my mom talking on the phone to her good friend, Gayle, who is an alcoholic but not a Catholic, which is confusing because I thought the two went together. Anyway, my mom said, "Screw guilt," to Gayle. I'm not really sure what that means, but I can only guess that it's probably a sin.

If there's one thing I noticed about being Catholic it's that Catholics are fueled by guilt. If we weren't filled up with guilt, we would feel happy. But we can't feel happy because there are too many starving children and sinners in the world, and we should just be happy and grateful for the food and family we have. Blah, blah, blah.

Sometimes, I would repeat this silly chant in my head that I made up when I was feeling bad about myself. It was rather disturbing at times, but it always reared its head when I got in trouble: "Mary, Mary, Mother of all, Tell me how many bad kids fall." I felt like I was one of the bad kids, even though I haven't broken any of the commandments yet.

In Catholic school and at my house, there weren't a lot of opportunities to feel good, to really feel like you were a good girl, a good person, or full of goodness. Mother Mary was full of goodness. She didn't look mean and unhappy like the nuns, either. I don't think she was ever a nun, but I don't know that for sure.

I first learned about Mother Mary officially in Kindergarten. But it took a few years for me to really connect with the fact that she is a real mother. Maybe it's because I've had such a hard time getting along with my real "Earth" mother... that's what I call my birth mom.

Every day in my school's morning mass service, I sit in a pew next to the Mother Mary statue. I confess I am guilty of daydreaming during mass. Sometimes I daydream that Mother Mary is my mother. Maybe it's because she's a mother and isn't holding a flyswatter.

I get in trouble sometimes in mass, but thankfully other students get in trouble, too. I'm glad I'm not the only kid in school who thinks mass is Boresville times infinity.

Once, Mary brought a really cool horse magazine to school so we took it to mass and hid it under the scriptural leaflet. But this fat, bald-headed dude took it from us and didn't even give it back after mass. The "parents' row" was right behind my class's row so we couldn't get away with too much bad stuff.

So on those bored days, I'd look up at Mother Mary's eyes and feel comforted by her outstretched arms with her dainty hands reaching out to me. The love in her eyes made her look so strong, yet sweet as her soft blue and white gown flowed gracefully over her tiny feet. She didn't have any nail polish on, though. That's the only thing I would add if I had built her statue.

My daily worshipping of the Mother Mary began innocently enough. I found a small, plastic statue of the Mother Mary in some bushes at the side of my house. It was like a miniature statue of the Mother Mary at my school sanctuary. Her hand was broken, though, like she was supposed to be holding something.

After I looked some more, I found the baby Jesus. It was like Mother Mary and baby Jesus were flying down from Heaven and landed in my yard! It was like Dorothy and the Wizard of Oz. And when they landed, the baby Jesus fell out of Mother Mary's arms, and it was my job to find him and put him back. I felt so important!

So I took the broken statue inside and glued the Mother Mary and the baby Jesus together. At night, I put my new statue in my God box that I kept under my bed.

Really early on Sunday morning, I wasted no time setting up an altar in the shelter of some marigolds I'd planted the spring before. I decided it would be my private sanctuary, a garden where I could talk to God and pray to a Mother who would listen and not yell at me or chase me around the house with a nasty flyswatter. I would pretend that God and Mother Mary were my real parents. I decided that, perhaps, I could know God, love him, and serve Him in a slightly different way. Instead of always being afraid of Him, like the nuns said we were supposed to. I wanted to stop being afraid. I just wanted to love Him.

But first, I decided that the Virgin Mary statue needed a makeover. I wasn't one to wear any makeup, but I decided that since the Virgin Mary was an adult woman that it would be OK.

So I found some pink lipstick from my mom's makeup drawer and put it on her lips. I added some blush like she was a paint by number picture, and a little bit of green eye shadow that my next door neighbor, Lorie, stole from the drug store. I think God already forgave her for stealing.

Sometimes I'll pull Mother Mary out of her box and pray to her. I'll pray for my older sister to stop being bad so I can stop paying for her sins. And I'll pray for my brother to be adopted by an international couple who live in a foreign country far, far away. And I'll pray for my dad to stop drinking. And I'll pray for the nuns to be nicer. And I'll pray for a new name and I'll pray to stop this ugly feeling I have inside that tells me I'm really supposed to be a boy.

I realize I'm supposed to be saying all this confession stuff to Father Flanagan during my weekly confessionals, but I don't think it's really any of his business. Plus, he's always liquored up so I don't think he really listens to these deep, dark secrets called confessions. Guilt makes for good job security for priests. Their confessionals will never go out of business as long as guilt is in.

I think at Catholic school, you're always supposed to feel bad so you don't do bad things. It's like a form of sin prevention.

Mary and I never really did anything bad, per se. I mean we would sneak out of her house when I spent the night sometimes. And there was the time Mary dared me to slide under all of the pews from the back to the front during mass one day. And the day that I wore my orange hip hugger bell bottom pants under my ugly plaid uniform. It was freezing outside and I was more concerned about keeping my legs from becoming Popsicle sticks.

And one time, we did steal unblessed hosts out of the sanctuary. But we were hungry so we didn't think it was really stealing and felt God would understand that we were starving. Besides, they didn't taste very good anyway.

Then, another time, we found a cigarette butt on the playground and it was actually Mary O'Donnell's idea to take it to the creek later and smoke it. Yuck! But later that afternoon, Sister Ann Dorez, our principal, got on the loudspeaker and announced that a cigarette butt had been found on the playground and that the playground police would find out who it belonged to. We didn't even know we had playground police!

But we believed the nuns because they do all kinds of mean things. Mary and I were convinced we were going straight to Hell without the option to confess, so she wadded it up in some notebook paper and threw it away.

I thought Sister Dorez's reaction was a bit hypocritical, though. One day after school, Mary and I saw her and Sister Mad smoking cigarettes behind the Kindergarten portables. It was Ash Wednesday, but that shouldn't make it OK to create ash. It was fun to watch the Sisters of St. Nicotine commit the sin of harming the temple that God created.

Another time we almost got in really big trouble. And it would have been my dad's fault.

One day at school, Mary Flaherty and I were asked to wash the chalkboards. So we got the pail of water from the girls' bathroom and started the long walk down the hallway back to our classroom.

"Wait a minute, Mary," I whispered. "I want to show you something cool that I learned from my dad's science fair." Actually it was an exhibit that my dad essentially did for me at last year's science fair on the subject of centrifugal force. Needless to say, I won another blue ribbon.

"Watch this," I tell Mary as I'm twirling the bucket of water faster and faster around and around with one arm. "See?" my whisper is growing louder. "It's centrifugal force!" I was beaming with the pride of my father.

The bucket of water is spinning faster and faster and out of control and then, *Splat!* Suddenly all of the water came crashing down in the middle of the hallway, forming a huge pond and drowning my saddle oxfords.

"Mary, run quick to the boys' restroom!" It happened to be closer than the girls' restroom. "Grab some paper towels!"

So we were both in the middle of the hallway, desperately praying the Hail Mary and the Our Father, hoping that no nun would grace the halls at that moment in time. My heart was beating so fast and I was starting to really sweat. And I never sweat. And then I realized it's not sweat, but water – and lots of it.

Within seconds, we had the pond sucked up with those heavy duty industrial nun-approved towels without a nun in sight! Whew!

"Great science project, Riley," snickered Mary.

"Well, it worked for a little bit. You got the idea."

I knew science would never be my thing.

Sometimes I guess me and my friends do stupid things, but at least we don't always get caught. Because if we got caught every single time, then that would qualify us as *really* bad. And really the only thing bad about me is my name. And only because the nuns think it's a boy name and they really don't like boys much because that's one of the reasons they became nuns. But my name is Irish so that helps a little because Father Flanagan is Irish and he's the nuns' boss.

But the nuns have more power.

The bell rang and it was off to lunch, my favorite time of day.

CHAPTER SIX

Food Police Destroys Food Psychic

At lunch, I rule.

The cafeteria is my domain. I am the lunch goddess. Well, not really a goddess. I'm more like a food psychic, but not like the fortune teller at the carnival. I make a point to memorize the lunch menus for each week so I know in advance if I need my mom to make a lunch for the next school day.

Word got around the school that I had ESP so students would call me at home to ask me what we were having for lunch the next day. There really was no secret or ESP thing about it. I was known as the Food Psychic, a title I was proud of and had fun playing along with it.

"Hi Riley. This is Mary," said the tender voice on the other end of the line.

"Mary who?" I responded.

"Mary Ochoa," she said.

"Oh," I said.

Silence.

It was Saturday evening so I knew it was a kid from school who wanted to know the future of her food week at school. I set strict ground rules for my psychic services: no calls on Sundays. My dad forbids phone calls on Sundays. He says that Sundays are God and family days... no friends, no calls, no fun, period.

"Well, Mary. Did you need something?" I asked kindly.

"Yeah, kinda," she spoke ever-so-softly with fear fumbling off her tongue. "I want to know what the cafeteria lady is gonna fix for lunch on Monday. I was told you are the Food Psychic and have the ESP." Her words stumbled with every exacerbated breath.

I should really charge big bucks for this special service.

She was so afraid that she sounded like she was about to have an asthma attack.

"Are you OK?" I asked as though I was now providing psychiatric services. She didn't say a word, but her breathing became more laborious. And then it occurred to me that the caller was the quiet Mary in fourth grade. Most of the Mary's are loud. I think they know they have all the power since their name is Mary. Power in numbers, they say.

"Um. Let's see. I can see clearly now. We are having… we are having… Monday at school our lunch will be… spaghetti," I professed with omnipotence.

"WOW! How do you do that?" Mary asked.

I wanted to be honest, I really did. No lie. But it was kind of fun playing a psychic, especially when we have a nun guarding the one and only trash can in the cafeteria.

"Are you afraid the nun food police will find out about your power and do something bad to you?" she asked with grave concern.

Nun police are everywhere and have specific titles describing their duties. The titles aren't official, but the word "police" is always used. What's funny, and sad, is that most kids are more afraid of nuns than police with guns.

"She can't punish me for having a sharp mind," I assured her, and wanted to add, *or for memorizing the weekly lunch menu that hasn't changed in the last six years.*

"If she does anything mean to you, you should report her to the Pope or somebody big like that." Mary spoke with the utmost conviction for a fourth grader, though she had a point.

The lunch nun food police really was a witch, and I really should report her. But to who? Another nun? Fat chance.

And she was the fattest nun at our school, standing right over the trash can daily like Great Britain's police force guarding the palace walls without cracking a smile, much less breathing. The designated Food Police, Sister Nehib, or, as we lovingly referred to her, Sister Body Parts.

When she first came to St. Paul's from Germany all the way to Texas, we heard the name "Knee Hip" over the announcement when she was introduced. Sister Marie Salvador reports the daily announcements and she is Hispanic with a very strong south of the border accent. Bless her heart. That's what all of the parents always say anyway.

Sometimes my menu memory backfired on me. I made the mistake of memorizing only the main entrée, like hamburgers or chicken fingers, which one first grader actually thought they were the fingers of actual chickens fried to a crisp. I reassured her and told her that chickens don't have fingers. There is a downside to being a Food Psychic.

I also hate the menu sometimes. For instance, I hate peas. Hate with the kind of passion that could make a kid vomit. And that's just what I do when I eat peas. Sister Food Police Detective is in charge of making sure the students eat *everything*, and I mean *everything*, on our plates.

Just out of mere survival, I trained myself to swallow one pea at a time like a pill and wash each and every pea down with my chocolate milk. But I always ran out of chocolate milk so some peas had to be squished between my teeth which made me gag.

So I became even cleverer. After drinking all of my milk and eating all of my food except those disgusting peas, I spooned those green balls of mush into my empty milk carton very methodically under the table so the nun police and tattle tellers couldn't see.

The disgusting pea squish was my motivation to become the food psychic with magical powers. The theory was this: if I knew what the lunch menu would be then I could bring my lunch and wouldn't get busted by the food nun-police detective. But I failed to memorize the "pea days." And that was a critical error.

As I entered the cafeteria, I immediately saw my Mary friends and felt relieved to finally be at lunch and out of the classroom.

"Hi Mary's!" I said with an emphasis on the plural. I noticed Mary O'Donnell and Mary Tierney sitting side by side looking very twin-ish. "Can I sit with y'all?" I asked.

"Sure, as long as you can give us the name of the company who makes these pukey peas so we can send hate mail to them," vocalized a highly-tempered Mary O'Donnell who was the extreme opposite of Mary Tierney, who was the congenial Irish redhead and class clown who has never met a stranger. That's what my dad says about people, Irish people in particular, who are super friendly.

Being the food psychic was fun, but it had its limitations. But soon someone would figure out that I don't have ESP and I don't have psychic power. They would figure out that it's the regular weekly lunch menu and then I'd be laughed at or worse, kicked out of jump rope club. I'm not very good at jumping rope anyway.

Or something even worse could happen, and it did.

I absolutely could not swallow another pea the next time they were served. And feeling the squish between my teeth was no longer an option. So I stashed the peas in my empty milk carton and walked my tray to the trash can that was heavily guarded by Sister Knee Hip who never smiles.

Normally I look Sister Knee Hip straight in the eyes and ask how her day is going. It can be a very effective diversion technique. It's not that I really care about her or how her day is going. It's more of a way to distract her from inspecting my tray for any remaining food particles that might be wasted. I bet she has a pair of night vision goggles, too, for her night time inspections.

But for some reason, I guess guilt had surfaced as I unknowingly bowed my head. That must have triggered an alert that screamed, "She's lying!"

And that's when the worst possible thing happened in my once worshiped and highly-respected domain.

Sister Knee Hip ordered me to hand her my milk carton which of course, was full of peas. My hand was shaking so bad that I "accidentally" dropped the carton in the trash can.

Deep breath. *Whew! That was close*, I thought to myself.

And then the gauntlet.

"Start digging!" she bellowed like a master grave digger in a frightening thriller working the night shift at the cemetery, and exactly where I felt I was going today after school… or possibly after lunch.

I pretended not to hear or understand her command.

"You heard me, Ms. Patton. And you have three seconds to dig that carton out of the trash can or you will suffer the consequences," she spoke as her evil flowed like lava.

Hmmmm.

I fearfully look up and ask, "What are the consequences?"

"The consequences, my dear, aren't pretty, nor are they fun."

I'm thinking, *OK Sister, spit it out.* In fact, I'm starting to get kinda mad which is scaring me.

"You will stand in the corner of the cafeteria tomorrow during the Kindergarten lunch period while balancing that same milk carton on your head."

"Will I still have to dig it out, or can I make one of the Kindergarten students do it for me?" It seemed like a logical question to me.

And then she pulled a whistle out of her ugly black robe and blew the sucker in my ear. That's child abuse. No question about that.

By that point, every student, every cafeteria lady, two janitors, and several parents who were there having lunch with their kids all stopped what they were doing and jerked their heads at the same time toward the trash can where I stood red and shaking next to Sister Whistle Blower. And it was there that I experienced my first real school-related humiliation and life-altering crisis of my childhood.

I should have dug it out when I had the chance, when fewer eyes were absorbing my stupidity and completely embedding such foolishness in their brains forever, already forming a deep memory of this very tragic event. I could even already hear the gossip and the rumors in the halls and the confessionals. They would have to confess the fact that they gossiped.

So I dug out the carton and handed the mess to Sister Knee Hip with grace.

And she shook the carton like a Christmas present hoping to guess its contents. But then I giggled because who would give her a Christmas present?

"That's quite a strange sound coming from a milk carton. Don't you agree, Ms. Patton?"

"It certainly is, Sister. I wonder what got in the carton when I accidentally dropped it into the trash can. That's just weird."

I was trying to save myself from further humiliation, annihilation, constipation, and every other kind of "tion" word.

47

She opened the carton and dropped her jaw. For a second, I thought she was gonna down the peas which would have been really sweet. But sweet is the last description I would use at this point in my life. Actually from that point on, I don't remember much of anything. Within seconds, I was yanked by the ear and practically thrown in Principal Sister Dorez's office.

Thank God she wasn't there. Must be Sister St. Nicotine Day and Sister Dorez is taking a smoke break behind the church rectory.

"Riley Patton, you will sit on the discipline bench until Sister Dorez returns. In the meantime, you will sit with your feet together and your hands placed squarely and evenly on your legs, and don't move a muscle, speak a word, or breathe any air."

Holy moly! She is on fire today!

"I am going to call your parents immediately and report your offense. You will await further punishment."

So I waited. And I waited. And waited some more.

And then, the bell rang and it was time to go home.

No Sister Dorez in sight. Didn't see Sister Knee Hip anywhere, either. I wasn't worried about my mom or dad being called because they never answer the phone. My mom doesn't even have a cell phone, and my dad always misplaces his.

I think I have been saved by the Almighty God in Heaven.

I need something I can call my own. That I can "win" honestly so I can feel proud about myself. I can't seem to get a boyfriend. But I want more than a boyfriend anyway. Plus, I guess I don't really rule at lunch, either. As long as those stupid cafeteria ladies keep serving squishy gross green peas, I don't stand a chance.

Maybe I should pray about my situation to Mother Mary. She would definitely understand. I only wish she would talk back.

CHAPTER SEVEN

Seven Sins and Counting

After my tragic carnival experience, I had a long, honest talk with myself. I secretly looked in my bathroom mirror and said to myself, "Riley, get a grip!" I finally accepted that Shawn was in love with my sister and not me. And that Shawn's younger brother was in love with me, but I wasn't in love with him. It was a mess, and I wanted no part of it. I decided it was time for a change.

As a fifth grader, though, there's not a whole lot I can change. Especially if you go to a Catholic preparatory school where your white knee-length all cotton socks are monitored and it's a sin to adorn your body with any kind of color at all, no makeup or jewelry. Not that I have any real jewelry. It was a stretch to sport my "I LOVE BOYS!" pin, I'll admit. I think the reason I wore it was because it had some color on it, and it was different. No one else had one. Or if they did, they weren't wearing it. And it's not really that I loved boys that much anyway.

In fact, sometimes I really hate boys, especially my brother. Sister Salvador told me once, "We're most like the ones we dislike." Scary thought. She's the closest thing I have to a female mentor. Not that I want to become a nun when I grow up. God forbid! I just want to be a nice and happy person. At the present time, however, I just don't understand how I'm supposed to feel as a girl. I don't feel girly. I hope when I get older I'll feel girly; then life will be less confusing.

My next door neighbor, Lorie Oldham, takes ballet lessons like twenty times a week. She says she's gonna be the star ballerina in *The Nutcracker* one day. Lorie goes to the public school down the street. She wears pink clothes and her mom lets her wear watermelon flavored lip gloss. She even has one of those big plastic doll model heads that you can practice styling hair and makeup on. It's way cool.

I was often jealous – one of the Seven Deadly Sins – of Lorie because she and her mom go shopping together every

Saturday. It wasn't because she got a lot of new clothes, or the fact that they had more money than my family and less kids. I was envious of how close she was with to her mother. I could tell they really loved each other. Lorie actually had a Barbie doll, too, that she would play dress up with. She was very much a girly girl, and I tried being more of a girl with Lorie constantly feeding me girly advice.

She even had a great idea once to wear a rosary like a necklace. I was brave, but not that brave, so I decided to wrap my rosary around my wrist to make it look like a bracelet. I thought it looked rather pretty, almost girly girl pretty. I felt terribly guilty, though. Maybe I decided to ask Father Tierney during my next confession if God was OK with me wearing my rosary like a bracelet, and if He is OK with that, I will ask him if I can wear it like a necklace, too. I think I will space out these special requests to God so He doesn't think I'm asking for too much or that I'm high maintenance or anything.

I don't want to wear makeup, though. My lips are so big that there's no way I'd ever put red lipstick on them, or anything shiny either because then they would look *really* huge! I get teased anyway about my lips. One day at recess, some kids chanted, "Riley has nigger lips! Riley has nigger lips!" I can't change the size of my lips. And I'm certainly not going to draw any more attention to them by adding bright red lipstick! No way, no how!

But I did start to feel what my "shoulder buddy" must feel like, and it didn't feel very good. A shoulder buddy is the kid that sits sideways to you in class. My shoulder buddy happened to be the only black student in the entire school. His name is Adam, and he's new to St. Paul's SCHO. I really like Adam and think he's way cool and really brave. Except I did a really stupid, mean thing to him the other day. I put a pencil in Adam's afro. He was sitting in front of me in math class and my pencil got real short from heavy usage and the eraser was completely shot because I am not a math person. I thought he would be able to feel it, but he didn't even move or flinch or anything. I forgot about it until the next day in math class when I asked Adam if I could borrow a pencil, preferably a short stubby pencil like Sister Mad's fingers.

So Adam turns around and whispers, "I really like you Riley and think you're a great friend but the pencil you're describing shot out of my afro when I was combing my hair this morning before school and landed in my little brother's oatmeal. So no, I don't have a pencil you can borrow."

And then I realized what "bad" was, so I apologized and said never mind on the pencil. I felt really bad because Adam is my friend. I just do stupid stuff sometimes.

How are we supposed to do good all the time if some things happen that make us feel bad? Adam is the only black kid in our school. He actually sits next to me in all of my classes, and our religion teacher, Mr. McNaughton, picks on him. Mr. McNaughton is called a "lay teacher" and he substitutes for the nuns from time to time. He actually scares me so I can only imagine how he makes Adam feel. Probably not very good at all.

Mr. McNaughton has brown curly hair – sort of like a white person's afro – and a grizzly-looking mustache that he's always pressing down with his thumb and forefinger. I guess the hairs must tickle his nose, or he has boogers or food in his 'stache.

He served two missions in Afghanistan and came back really angry, and he never smiles. I think he hates black people, too, because he's always yelling at Adam for little things like not pushing his chair in when we leave the classroom.

One day, Adam asked if he could use the restroom, but he forgot to raise his hand first. So Mr. McNaughton started poking Adam in the chest real hard with his mustache finger and yelled, "No Adam, you cannot use the bathroom, and, 'why is that?' you must be thinking. It's very simple, Adam. You must raise your hand first and then wait on me to finish my lecture. But oh, no, your need to relieve yourself is more important than getting a good education. So here's the deal. You're going to sit there for the rest of class with your feet flat on the ground and both hands flat on your desk, and sit perfectly still without speaking a word."

All the way through this verbal beating, I sat there frozen stiff at my desk mimicking Adam's every move, setting my breathing in rhythm with his and feeling every ounce of fear. And then it hit me. I got it, and I DID NOT like it one bit. It's discrimination and it's a sin.

I wanted to cry for Adam and for all the black people in the world. At the same time, I wanted to punch Mr. McNaughton in the face, break his fifties-style glasses, poke his eyes out with my forefinger and rip off that stupid mustache of his. It's probably fake anyway.

But all I could do was breathe. My heart was pounding so hard like an alien was about to launch from my chest.

I could also hear Adam's heart beating, or breaking into little pieces. I knew mine was. I now understood the phrase, "killing the human spirit."

Mr. McNaughton was a cold, heartless, spirit-killer. And a sinner at that.

We have another lay teacher at SCHO. Her name is Mrs. Boswell and she's Adam's aunt, which is how Adam got accepted to our SCHO. She's super nice to all of us, even Mr. McNaughton. I don't know how she's able to stop herself from taking Mr. McEvil all the way to the Supreme Court.

Mrs. Boswell went to college with my dad. My dad isn't a hater, but I'm pretty sure my mom is. She calls Hispanics "Mexticans," with emphasis on the "t." I'm not sure why, though. But Kat had a boyfriend one time named Gerald Lopez who my mom called a Mextican when she yelled at Kat non-stop for five days straight. It was my mom's plan to "break her spirit" at home while Sister Peg Leg broke her spirit at school in order to force Kat and Gerald to break up.

After school, I told Adam about the ear plugs I have to wear whenever I go swimming. I get ear aches really bad so the doctor makes me wear these really huge and very ugly ear plugs which make me look like a really old person. One time when I was kinda in the deep end of the pool, the lifeguard started waving his arms at me like he was a clapping monkey or something. I thought what a weirdo. And then, he got off his lifeguard duty chair and walked over to me at the edge of the pool and started doing some kind of hand gestures. It was then that I realized not only do I look like an old person with these stupid ear plugs, but this lifeguard thinks I'm deaf so he's trying to tell me something in sign language.

That was a first.

I looked at him, and as loud as I could, I yelled, "I can hear moron!" which made him fall back from his squatting position on the side of the pool. I started laughing and so did some other kids around me which made me feel better and far less humiliated. Mr. Lifeguard apologized and sternly told me to get out of the deep end.

Now he must think I can't swim.

For the sake of my own sanity, I swam back over to the other end of the pool, climbed out and headed toward the girl's restroom so I could cry. I'm not normally so emotional and I absolutely hate – and I mean *hate* – crying, especially in public or around Kat and her friends or at school or the mall. Basically everywhere. When I got home, I put my ear plugs in an empty potato chip bag and threw the bag in the trash.

I also went straight to our "teen computer" and researched sign language. I was determined to become an expert sign language person so I could talk to deaf people, young or old, so they won't feel like people are making fun of them.

That was something I could change. I wasn't so sure about my new haircut, though. But it was something else I could change, too. The short bob may be a bit too tomboyish. But it's starting to grow on me. Well, not really grow. But after looking in the mirror about three thousand times without throwing up or feeling nauseated, I felt like I could get used to it.

I know a lot of girls who, if they get dumped, feel like their life is over. One girl last year (I think her name was Mary Wheelan) wouldn't eat for a week when her boyfriend broke up with her. A whole week! No fries! No pizza! Nothing! No boy is worth that sacrifice, that's for sure! And it's not like I really got "dumped" because Shawn and I were never going together. It was a silent break up which hurt, but not so much that the whole school knew about it.

I feel spring coming on, anyway. I need to do what my mom calls, "Spring Cleaning," but the funny thing is I don't ever see her cleaning. She just has her kids do all the work. I can't wait to be a grown up. Then I will have more answers.

Whenever I travel with Mary Flaherty and her family, boys would always flirt with her. They never flirt with me. They always ask me her name. Mary is a girly tomboy. She is little and has a few curls that fluff up her light brown hair. But she likes to gallop her horse and poach frogs, too.

"Riley, phone call!" yelled my mom from downstairs.

"Who is it?" I yelled in response.

"It's Mary."

"Mary who?"

"Mary Flaherty, your best friend. Who else?"

My mom didn't go to Catholic school so she's clueless to the problem of the multiple Mary's.

"Hi Mary, what's up?" I casually ask.

"Hey, the altar boy, I mean, altar boy girl tryouts are next Tuesday and I want us to try out together because you have to try out with a partner."

"What?!" I yelled.

"Well, it doesn't have to always be boys," reasoned my best and smartest friend, Mary Flaherty. "None of the fifth grade boys are gonna try out anyway so we might as well," she said.

She had a good point. And it was time for me to expand my horizon, stretch my wings, open my mind, and get a grip. It was time for me to make an honest name for myself and show my true leadership abilities at my school. A girl doesn't have to have a boyfriend to feel important or cool.

But then I thought... it always gets me down when I think too much.

"But I don't want to be a priest when I grow up, Mary," I confessed.

"Riley! You don't have to be a priest just 'cause you're an altar boy, I mean girl," she said.

"Oh. Well, then OK. I'm in!" I said with the kind of excitement I hadn't felt since I won Most Valuable Player on my soccer team. So we marched right into Father Tierney's rectory and asked him for the sign-up sheet for the altar boy girl tryouts.

"Excuse me?" I said to Father Tierney, who lowered his spectacles, rolled his eyes, and begged a look that could have broken our spirits, but we pressed forward as the determined history makers we were.

Father Tierney cleared his throat, returned his eyeballs to their straight forward position after a few rolls around their sockets, and quietly instructed us to proceed with writing our names on the tryouts sign-up sheet under the column, "Boy's Name."

I then proceeded to correct Father Tierney and remind him we are girls, and that there needs to be a "Girl's Name" column on the sign-up sheet. At that point, he took a big gulp of wine like it was a Slurpee and looked at us like we were challenging the Pope, so we just walked away before he called some of the nuns in to swat the tops of our hands with rulers.

Mary and I hurried out of the rectory office like we were holding our breath and shut Father Tierney's door, then turned to each other and grinned so wide it felt like my smile was touching my ear lobes.

Then Mary and I did something we hadn't done since we stayed the night with her family at a KOA campground promising to be best friends forever: we did our "pinky power" handshake.

CHAPTER EIGHT

Altar Girls Altering History

"We are so awesome!" Mary beamed after we hooked our pinky fingers together to solidify our plan. We "kiss our brain" after we pinky promise shake using our pinky fingers when we come up with a great plan. Kissing your brain simply means you kiss your pinky and then touch the top of your head. Sister—I mean—*Mrs*. Abbott taught us how to do it when we made a good grade on a test. It's become a part of our ritual in our Mutual Admiration Society. She's the co-president and I'm the co-president, and we're the only kids in the club. It's our "think pink power" girls only club.

"We could be the first altar girls ever in the history of St. Paul's," I shared with excitement as Mary walked down the hall. "I love making history, especially when you don't have to get in trouble to make it."

"Hey, let's go to the computer lab and Google altar girl gowns and find out what styles they come in."

"Great idea, Mary. We have to look good, after all. We'll probably be in the newspaper," I said with pride.

We noticed Ms. Fleming, the substitute teacher, in the computer lab.

"Can we pleeeease use one computer, Ms. Fleming?" I asked ever so sweetly.

Mary and I held our pinky fingers up together as if raising the American flag. Ms. Fleming is so cool. She's young and knows the "think pink" girls club code. We had to tell her about it one time and she promised with her pinky not to tell any of the nuns.

As she smiled in response to my question, she turned the lab light back on and said, "OK, girls. But only for five minutes. I have to help Sister Dorez wax the pews."

What an unpleasant task, I thought to myself. Ms. Fleming is way too good for this school.

"White, white, and more white," I said with a tone of frustration. "Why all the white? How boring!"

"Wait a minute," said Mary with an ounce of hope. "Here's an 'ivory.'"

"Oh, that sounds even better. That will look beautiful against our ivory skin," my reaction was a bit sarcastic, but Mary smirked with the understanding of best friends. What did we really expect to find? Swatches of floral, pastels, plaids, and polka dots? It's not like we were the fashion queens of the school anyway.

"Well, white is OK," I said settling for the only true option available when both of us really wanted pink gowns that we could ask my neighbor to embroider our initials on the front of.

"White is kinda like a wedding gown though, don't ya think?" Mary looked concerned.

"Sister Salvador told me one time that she married God and was 'at peace' with her decision. I wonder if she wore a wedding gown on that day."

"Maybe we can wear some pretty earrings or at least some kind of head band or something colorful and cool," said bright-eyed Mary so full of illusions.

"Yeah, right," I said sarcastically. "We'll be lucky if they let us wear floral print underwear…. Well, how 'bout a watch with a designer band," I added, sounding a bit more hopeful yet just as unrealistic.

"At least we won't have to wear a habit!" smiled Mary, and then we both started laughing at the thought of walking down the aisle in a nun habit.

Two very long weeks later, the results were in. I'm not sure what the trouble was or why it took so long because there were only six of us trying out. The other pairs were both boys and were very sloppy with Father Tierney's wine and actually spilled some of it on their white robes which made it look like blood. Of course, the boys thought it was cool, but I could see Sister Mad's face flame a bright red like a fire truck on duty. She's in charge of all laundry for the church and school, and proper order of the utility room which doesn't have any of that fancy stain-be-gone spray.

Finally, Father Tierney posted the list of winners in order of first, second and third. I felt like I was a racehorse at the Kentucky Derby except it was the altar kid derby. And I wasn't a horse, but I sure felt as powerful as one and power feels pretty darn good, I must say.

"Riley Patton (girl)" and Mary Flaherty (girl)" was smack dab at the top of the list. I could hardly contain my excitement. Mary and I looked at each other and started hugging each other and crying happy tears. I grabbed Mary's hand and walked as fast as I could to the nearest girl's bathroom, slid into the closest open stall, flushed the toilet, and we let out the biggest "BOO-YAH" (which means "in your face"... actually it's a thick soup of unknown origin made in the Midwestern United States) we could without alarming the closest nun on bathroom duty.

Without a doubt, today is the best day of my life!

CHAPTER NINE

The "Big Four" is Not a Basketball Tournament

I can't understand why nuns wear black, if indeed they are supposed to be a happy bunch blessed with God's graces and all. After all, their long and thick black robes cover every inch of glorious skin that the good Lord made. Why don't they wear white, if they're supposed to be so pure? Black is so depressing. But black makes perfect sense for nuns like Sister Mad and Sister Peg Leg who probably don't have people skin and the reptile ridges on their arms would show though white robes.

I just figure the mean nuns have scarlet leather skin that resembles the devil, or at the very least perhaps the skin of a reptile, all thick, bumpy, and ugly. My best friend, Mary, said she should donate her skin to a boot company when she dies so they can make those fancy alligator skin boots. She is a Texas nun, after all. I decide that if I live through this Catholic school thing, then I am going to free all of the nuns from their misery when I get older. I'm not sure how I will do that, but I feel certain they will thank me later.

A few years after the opening of St. Paul's School, the Benedictine Sisters from Illinois came to staff the school and served St. Paul's until the heavy irons were called in. The Sisters of Notre Dame replaced the Benedictine Sisters and have remained the upper hand of Godly guidance until today.

Early on, the school used the auditorium for a church sanctuary, parish hall, and cafeteria. Some old barrack buildings were purchased from the local Air Force Base to make more room for more students because the school was getting so popular. I'm not sure why, though... I don't understand why parents would want their kids to go to a school that costs a lot of money and has evil nuns as teachers. I'm sure I will never do that to my kids when I grow up.

The Sisters of Notre Dame were big on virtues. The "Big Four" virtues, that is. Every lesson, with the exception of math, the Sisters included the Cardinal Virtues we know as prudence, temperance, justice, and good ole fortitude.

Prudence was kind of like the word sounded, prudish. Actually, prudence meant that you had common sense. We learned that it was when you actually took the time to think out what you are doing and what is likely to come of it. It was a behavior-consequence lesson, essentially. I think Kat needs more prudence in her lessons.

Temperance was used to describe our uniform dress length, our hair length (bangs), our appetite, and the s-word. We were taught that temperance meant that you go the right length and no further. In other words, know your limits and stick with them no matter who is trying to hold your hand at the school carnival and other horrible acts of human sexuality.

I think I need more temperance for my bangs. My mom never takes us to a real hair salon because it costs too much money, so she cuts our hair herself. Sometimes she gets too busy and doesn't realize that my bangs are so long they are touching the tip of my nose. I guess I could point this aversion out to her but I hate it when my mom cuts my hair. My bangs are always crooked and way too short when she cuts them. One time my mom cut Danny's ear lobe when she was cutting his hair and he bled and cried for a whole day. I actually felt sorry for him for the first time in my life, and his, too.

Sister Mad scolded me one time as we lined up for recess.

"Ms. Patton!" she bellowed like a hot air balloon on fire.

I thought to myself, *What in Sam Hill have I done now?* I'm not sure what Sam Hill means but my mom says it all the time. I think Sam Hill must have been an old boyfriend of hers that dumped her, or possibly a child she gave up for adoption because she realized she gave birth way too many times.

"Yes, Sister," I replied like a good girl, which was very difficult but required when Sister Mad gets that tone in her voice. Sometimes I wonder when the nuns are gonna handcuff the sinning students and lock us up in the broom closet.

"I want you to get your scissors from your locker and walk immediately to the school nurse's office to reconcile the inappropriately long bangs you are wearing. I will call your mother this afternoon regarding this matter," said a very mad Sister Mad.

"OK," I said as though I was happy about the whole situation.

Behind my bangs was my brain thinking, *I would rather get my bangs cut by the school nurse using my dull elementary school scissors than my mom when I get home.* Plus, I wasn't afraid about Sister Mad calling my mom because my mom always sleeps in the afternoons, and our phone doesn't have a voice message so it rings and rings, which never wakes up my mom because she's so sad most days and sleeps right through the rings.

I like going to the school nurse. Her name is Mrs. Strayhan. Her husband was a famous football player but now he's retired because he got hurt way too many times. Mrs. Strayhan volunteers because she doesn't need money since her husband made so much when he played football, even though they had five kids. Sometimes I just go to her office just to be near her and talk. She's easy to talk to. She seems really happy even though she has five kids.

Justice, the next virtue, was easy. It's not a lawyers and order in the court kind of thing. Justice simply meant that you keep your promises. Sort of like when my BFF Mary and I do our pinky promise thing. We always keep our promises to each other, unlike most adults. When I get to be an adult, I'm always going to keep my promises.

The last virtue is Fortitude. Just the word itself means serious business. Fortitude was about courage, actually two kinds of courage: facing painful people and uncomfortable situations, like being alone in a room with more than one nun. I think I should receive the badge of courage just by surviving life in my house, and facing the nuns on a daily basis. Having good friends and a school nurse who is easy to talk to helps a lot.

When St. Paul the Apostle Preparatory School of Catholic Higher Order first opened, it was called the White Settlement Mission School. I can only suppose that no blacks were allowed. I often wondered if the nuns made that rule. I've never seen a black nun, either. I wonder if the black nuns wear white robes and white habits. I wonder where the black nuns teach and why we can't have black nuns.

I think there should be a fifth virtue called Fairness. My dad always says, "Life isn't fair so get over it." I wonder sometimes if that's why he drinks so much.

The year SCHO opened its doors, there were only 22 kindergartners and 39 first graders. It gradually expanded to include second grade through sixth grade. After sixth grade, then the girl students graduate to Our Lady of Victorious (OLV) and the boy students are sent to St. Jude's School.

Kat's at OLV and I'm glad. Since I'm a tomboy, I wonder if I will go to OLV or St. Jude's. If I had my way, which I never do, I would go to public school.

St. Jude is the patron saint of hopeless causes, which was my take on most boys exactly. The separation into singular genders was to, "respect the purity of our hearts," as stated in our school brochure. The gender separation was constantly reiterated by the nuns, especially when they catch a boy and a girl making out like my sister and Shawn. Automatically, however, the nuns suspect that I'm just as bad as my sister as though badness is genetic and runs through family blood.

At St. Paul's, both boys and girls had to wear a uniform. But the boys got off easy with khaki pants and a white button down shirt. The boys weren't tethered to a uniform tie until they reached St. Jude's in the seventh grade.

One year, a group of parents of St. Jude boys fought the Establishment and petitioned for a more "relaxed" uniform; relaxed was also known as "civvies." The girls in particular longed to be liberated from the oppression of the plaid uniform look as well, but we knew better than to protest. Plaid, to me, was a boy's style. Maybe that's why I felt more boyish.

For the girls, OLV did allow khaki pants in addition to the plaid skirt and bib. I was relieved because the cold winter months were difficult without pants or leggings. Plus, pants were a little easier during that time of the month, based on what my sister and her friends said.

To survive Catholic school, you have to learn how to code and classify. A sense of humor is also extremely vital. Mary and I have classified the nuns in our school. We have the "fun nuns" like Sister Marie Salvador, who is so sweet and younger than the others. She talks with a funny accent and we love listening to her talk about her family in Mexico. I want to visit there one day, maybe even go on a mission trip to Mexico with my church's youth group. Next are the "St. Nicotine Nuns" like Sister Dorez and Sister Mad. We realize there is no such person as St. Nicotine, but it helped us justify and accept nun smokers.

Then, we have the "Evil Ones" like Sister Peg Leg, and Sister Mad also fits in that category. She just needs to retire. Mary and I also figured out that the mean nuns don't die. They don't have souls, either, like me and Mary and other human people. You can dispel them for a while, maybe even for a lifetime if you're Irish and lucky. But they are primal forces. Archetypes like St. Michael, the archangel. But they are arch-devils. Eventually, they re-form into new and even more evil monsters.

Every Friday at St. Paul's, the entire school has to go to mass. After mass, the upper grades have to rotate confession. It's really more like drive through confessional because we're actually timed. Father Tierney sits in the confessional with a kitchen timer. Some Fridays, I run out of stuff to confess so I just make it up.

Sister Mad says it's "our duty" to confess our sins in a timely manner. But what if you lie in confession about what your sins are? I'm not sure what the punishment is for that. I might just confess that one today.

I think being forgiven is like having mud all over your body and then you get to take this warm, sudsy shower bath both at the same time so the clean water can wash away all the mud.

The Holy Spirit is probably much more forgiving than the Holy Ghost who doesn't sound like he'd be the friendly kind.

CHAPTER TEN

The Sacrament of Giving Up Candy
and Possibly Boys, Too

We have to give up candy every year for Lent.

I have to be very honest. It isn't as hard as it seems. We never get much candy to begin with so it's not like I'm giving up a daily thing. In fact, I used to get more candy at school than at home until they passed the new "no sweets" law forbidding sweets at school. I'm sure it was a nun who came up with that stupid law. I must admit, though, it would be hard to give up jalapeños. The first time I bit into a jalapeño I was only five. And it wasn't the chocolate covered jalepeño variety.

My dad's friend, "Mr. Bummer," told me it was a "Texas pickle." So I did a very foolish thing and believed him. And then I took a big Texas bite. I pretended that the burning sensation was not a big deal. But deep inside, I felt like my throat was bleeding.

I didn't feel like it was really a lie, but I did feel like I was going to burn in hell for it. Or actually, I was already burning on Earth paying for my sin of lying. I guess I could confess to the Lent Police. I'm not sure who that would be, though. That part isn't in the Bible. I think next year I will give up anything hot for Lent, just to protect myself from people like Mr. Bummer who I once thought was so funny and nice.

Coffee seems to be the most popular Lenten sacrifice. My mom gives up coffee for Lent. My dad gives up beer and drinks more coffee, for about a week. We don't eat meat on Fridays during Lent, either. My mom makes these really gross fish sticks. We have to dip them in lots of ketchup to disguise the taste.

I thought about giving up boys for Lent, but that wouldn't be considered a real sacrifice since I don't even have a boyfriend. But I was thinking about a boy and that is the same thing as having a boyfriend, at least when you're a Catholic because if you lust in your head then it's the same thing as doing it for real. This particular sin never made a lot of sense to me since it was just a thought and I didn't really *do* anything with it.

I guess I will have to give up my thoughts of Shawn. I need to write that in my Mad/Sad/Glad Father God and Mother Mary journal. It doesn't have a lock, though, so I have to hide it really well.

But I wanted to have a boyfriend because a new boy started school this week and he isn't even an Army brat. He's a real kid who might stay longer than a year, which seems like a really long time, but really isn't. I didn't mean that Army brats aren't real kids because they are. They just have so many rules and I have a hard time keeping up with their Army rules *and* the Nun rules at school. I'm constantly afraid I'm breaking a rule and not knowing it, and then something bad will happen. My friends who live on the Air Force Base have a curfew. They have to be in bed by 10pm, or at least off the streets and the playground. One time me and Irene fried an egg on the slide. Actually, it was more like five eggs because I remember now she got in trouble. Eggs and bacon. Parents should just accept that kids are going to fry eggs on the playground slides and use bacon to catch crawdads so they should buy extra eggs and plenty of bacon. My Army friends shop on base at the BX. Things are cheaper at the BX, but not bacon and eggs for some reason.

The new boy at my school is Liam O'Malley and he's from Ireland. Actually he told our class that his family stopped off in New York for a little bit. He's the real deal as my dad said. My dad said that all his daughters should marry an Irish man because the Irish are a passionate bunch who honor family. I said, "Then you should honor our family if you're really Irish." With that, I got slapped upside the head.

Liam is in my grade, too, which is good, but he doesn't have any younger brothers or sisters, which is bad. But he's real nice and real friendly and he even said hi to me today at lunch. I wonder if he knows I'm the lunch goddess. He would probably think that's stupid.

When I get home from school, I'm going to Google Irish food and ask my mom to take me to the store to buy something green so I can wear it to school tomorrow. Although I don't know what I can wear that's green. I can't even wear green eye shadow, but I don't need it because my eyes are green so I never get pinched on St. Patrick's Day, which is coming up real soon. I think I will also make an Irish lunch so I can sit by Liam and he might think I eat Irish food every day because I'm so Irish. Food and friendship go together you know.

I told Mary about my idea about cooking some Irish food. She's not Irish and asked if she could eat it if she's not Irish. I had to look that up, too. Corned beef and cabbage seem to be the main ingredients for Irish recipes which sounds completely disgusting so I will just dye my fried bologna sandwich green. Sort of like Green Eggs and Ham.

I think the green sandwich trick worked because Liam gave me a Claddagh ring after school. A Claddagh ring is like an Irish promise ring. I'm not sure what I am promising but I can promise to wear it until I don't like Liam anymore, which will probably be never because I am 100% sure that we are going to get married.

I kinda made a fool of myself after he gave me the ring. I was so happy that I tripped over my backpack that should have been on my back but it was on the floor next to my open locker. I was so embarrassed, but I didn't care 'cause I was more happy than embarrassed. Plus, Liam reached out his hand to help me up like a real prince and I was his princess. He even kissed my hand next to where my Claddagh ring was. I felt all tingly inside. I'm starting to feel things I've never felt before and I wonder if it's good or bad.

Oh, why do things always have to be either good or bad?

CHAPTER ELEVEN

"Pretend Praying" – It's All in the Timing

I'm in love.

It's all I think about. I mean, Liam and I getting married is all I think about. But I don't tell anyone, except my friend Irene and Mary Carter. I told Irene because I want her to tell her brother, Shawn, that I have a boyfriend now and don't care about him anymore. But that's not really the whole truth. It's part lie, too. I will have to confess all my partial lies in confession this Friday. I wonder how many of my partial lies add up to whole lies? I may have to lie about that, too.

It's weird being in love because I've never felt this feeling before. I can't even do my homework. I draw hearts in my math book. I created a new mathematical formula and it's Riley + Liam = Love. Since this is my last year of SCHO, I don't worry about vandalizing a school book. It's not really vandalizing anyway because it's about love and God said to love one another.

But I'm pretty sure he didn't say love one another by marking up the $36 math textbook. I heard the nuns make the vandalizers pay a fine, and they have to immediately go to confession. But most of the time, the nuns can't find Father Tierney. And then the nuns start mumbling under their breath and some let out a few un-nun-like words.

I wonder to myself, why can't a nun fill in for the priest? I mean, nuns will certainly dish out the penance. Father Tierney always gives out the penance of saying the Our Father five times and the Hail Mary four times. But how is he gonna know how many times the sinners pray? I mean it's not like we have to recite the prayer penance orally to a nun to prove we are actually serving our time.

I decided to time my penance one day to just see how long it should take an average kid, not that I'm average, but I read fast and daydream, too, so it averages itself out. It turns out that the average penance takes 4 minutes and 26 seconds. So I'm gonna set my new watch that Liam gave me the next time we have to go to confession and sit in the pew daydreaming about me and Liam.

His parents must be loaded. I like my new watch. The band is pink which makes me feel like a girly girl. The number six is actually a heart which beats along with the seconds that tick. I figured it takes 4 minutes and 26 seconds to say the 9-prayer penance. So after about five minutes, I make the sign of the cross and scoot out of the pew. I probably should feel a bit guilty for lying about my prayer penance, but I don't.

Since Father Tierney is oozing with booze as he stumbles through the sentencing, I pretend like I can't understand him anyway. I think God is madder at Father Flanagan than me for not really saying my prayers of confession.

Father Flanagan went to school with my dad. Not grade school, but The Seminary. You have to put the "The" in front of the word "Seminary" because it is a holy word. My Scotch and Water Granny wanted my dad, her only son, to become a priest.

So my dad did as ordered because he was too scared to disobey his mother, even though she was drunk most of the time just like Father Flanagan. My dad didn't make it, though.

He got kicked out of the holy school because he "partied" too much.

I'm not really sure exactly what that means, but it doesn't sound like a bad thing. I mean a party is a birthday party where people are happy and open presents and eat cake and ice cream and swing at piñatas filled with gummy candy that sticks to your teeth that the dentist complains about.

Sister Mad was spying on me the next day at confessional. She asked me why I watched my watch the whole time I was saying my prayer penance. I lied and told her I was doing math on it and then she got excited, but not really the normal people kind of excited, but a nun kind of excited. The side of her lip quivered slightly and her red pitchforks irises shaded to a light pink for a brief moment. I could actually see a real human in there. I couldn't believe my eyes!

So the next day, Sister Mad told Sister Salvador to make an announcement that students could start wearing watches, which was HUGE because jewelry of any kind was critically forbidden for generations of Catholic school history. But Sister Mad told us that watches are math tools.

Mary Flaherty, my best Mary friend, said she wanted a watch just like mine which didn't make any sense because you're not supposed to buy a heart watch for yourself. But she said it didn't matter because she loved my watch so that was that. I was curious, which always sets me down a bad path but I can't help myself. I wondered where Liam bought my watch and how much money he spent on it.

So I did the unheard of thing and asked him. My mom found out later and told me that it is rude to ask people how much money they spend on gifts. So I got grounded for the weekend but I asked her if I could just do the dishes instead and she said OK.

Ahh, the art of negotiation. I am good at this. It feels good to be good at something. It's probably not the real kind of negotiation because it's my mom and she's so exhausted most of the time, so that enhances my ability to manipulate her which strengthens my negotiation skills.

It turns out that Liam didn't know how much the watch was. He said he bought it at the BX which is the base super store. I'm not sure why it's called a "super" store because it's smaller than a normal person's – "civilian" – store. I think it has something to do with the military and the guns they carry, but they don't sell guns at the BX, only water pistols.

"How can you not know how much my watch was," I asked Liam like I was a mean nun or something. I'm scared I'm becoming one of them.

"I don't know. I didn't pay attention to the price," grumbled Liam. His tone took a twisted turn that showed a mean side I'd never seen before with a look that nipped at my heart. I guess everyone has a mean side, even boyfriends.

I could only assume that his parents had so much money that it didn't matter how much things cost. So I asked my mom how much she thinks a watch should cost and she said about $15 to $25 for a child's watch. I showed her my watch for the very first time, and she gasped.

"Where did you get that watch, Riley Patton?"

"Why, what does it matter?" I retorted. "Plus, it's not really a watch 'cuz Sister Mad said it was a math tool now."

"Riley," my mom said again and again. And makes the sign of the cross and mumbles some gibberish prayers like it's going to prevent me from going to you-know-where.

"I won it at the school carnival, don't you remember, mom?" I answered like a good girl telling one of those good kind of lies. I'm lucky because my mom doesn't have a very good memory because she has too many kids and a husband who likes beer.

CHAPTER TWELVE

My Very First Real Boyfriend
Turned Out to be a Criminal

I'm not sure how parents work behind the scenes, but it turns out my mom called Liam's parents to report the rather expensive gift their son gave me.

Just my luck. It turns out my first boyfriend is a liar and my first gift from my first boyfriend was stolen. A liar and a thief.

Apparently Liam stole the watch from the BX which was valued at approximately $75. I should have known it was too good to be true. So my parents made me return the watch and break up with Liam. I was humiliated and felt so sorry for Liam. He said he wanted to get me the best watch in the store because I was the best girlfriend he ever had. I will remember that forever when we talk next, but that may be a long time because his parents returned his cell phone. They said he will have plenty to talk about to Father Tierney in Friday confessional this week.

But by Friday, Liam was no longer a student of SCHO. The nuns voted to kick him out. Heartless. Back to public school for him. He's so lucky. Not really lucky, but I would give anything not to be at the mercy of nuns all day every day. So I'm back to square one. Riley, the boyfriend-less girl. But that's okay. I wouldn't want to be married to a criminal so it's a good thing the truth came out sooner rather than later. I'd hate to explain to my kids why their daddy is in prison.

My mom said from now on, she is going to "approve" who my boyfriends are.

"What? Are you kidding me?" I quivered at the thought of my own mother interviewing my future boyfriends like they were applying for a job or something. I admit I can be a lot of work, but geez.

"From now on, Riley, no boys. Period," my mom ordered, just like a nun. I could see the pitchforks in her eyes now. And I wonder if my mom was a nun in her former life.

"You'll be much better off without a boyfriend, especially one who breaks commandments." She was *filled* with knowledge of the Catholic laws.

The next day at school, Sister Peg Leg actually reported Liam's sin to the entire student body through the morning announcements. She instructed all of us to pray for his evil ways. Sometimes I think nuns enjoy the sinning of others, which seems very evil.

The thing is I couldn't understand why Liam would steal when his parents were rich. I thought only poor people and drug addicts took things that didn't belong to them. If I were rich, I'm pretty certain I wouldn't steal. I would give some to the poor people and keep the rest for my escape from my own prison, my home.

Because of Liam, the entire school had to write a 500-word essay on the 7th commandment "Thou shall not steal." But I didn't mind writing 500 words because I like to write and I still love Liam. So I drew 500 hearts on my paper, too.

It appears I have been alienated by the entire student body because of the "guilt by association" thing. But I'm not mad at Liam. He just does bad things like my sister Kat sometimes. But I *am* mad at her. I'm a permanent kind of mad at her. I can forgive Liam.

It's not that I forgive him for the total humiliation I am suffering because of his criminal behavior. That will take time. But I think I will give up boys for Lent. I told Sister Mad about my decision and she smiled so big I got scared.

I REALLY need a hobby. I think it would help me stop obsessing about Liam and his lying ways. And just stop thinking about boys in general. I started playing softball this past summer on a team that was coached by my friend's mom. She's a public school friend and I don't think her mom likes me. I sit on the bench at every single game. I wanted to quit so badly, but my mom yelled at me and said, "You will NOT quit!"

I could join the Peace Corps or something, without brothers and sisters and nuns and parents and lying boys. I'd probably have to move to another country because they probably have less people; that means fewer criminals and mean people in general, like nuns.

CHAPTER THIRTEEN

Sister Washyamouthoutwithsoap
and Other Hygiene Topics

I became a "woman" today at school, and the experience was absolutely awful. I hate that word, "woman," and I also hate the words, "menstrual cycle."

I started my period and was scared to death someone would find out. I was so freaked out for some weird reason. It should be called, "exclamation point," not just, "period." I'm gonna keep it a secret from my mother for at least a year. I'll just use her maxi-pads that she keeps under the bathroom sink. It was a great plan until the day I was invited to a swimming party by my friend, Kelly, who introduced me to the all-powerful tampon. Kelly is my public school friend who lives on my street. She has older sisters so she is very knowledgeable about woman stuff. I don't trust my sister Kat, and I certainly can't talk to my own mother because she's way too busy and distracted with her own life.

"Menstrual cycle" were two feared words in St. Paul's sex education course. The first course of its kind in the history of St. Peter, I sat in the class one hour each week turning red at every slide and too embarrassed to look any of my classmates in the eye. I'm pretty sure we all felt the same thing and just never talked about it. And that was part of the problem: we didn't talk about sex, or the menstrual cycle for that matter. We were merely receivers of information. We had our scheduled library time right after our sex education class, which became the perfect escape to get lost in the mountain of books.

On the day I started my period, I was at recess playing a jacks and ball game with Irene Bastrop. Irene was my best friend in the fifth grade, and she had the fastest "ball and jack" hand in the entire school, which meant I usually lost. I was so grateful that God had sent me a new friend whose name wasn't Mary. Irene came to St. Paul's by way of the military at the nearby Carswell

Air Force Base in Fort Worth. But I couldn't get real close to my Carswell friends because I had learned that they stay for one year and then move to another place.

I felt something wet in my panties and ran to the restroom, with permission of course. I was aghast but thought quickly. I would just wad up a bunch of toilet paper and pray for 3 pm to come faster than normal that day. I really wished for long pants, or even shorts, to wear under my uniform.

I told no one about this major change of life event, except for Kelly because I had to go to her swimming party, but I'm not gonna even tell my new best friend Irene or even Kat because I know Kat would tell all of her friends and make fun of me. I certainly couldn't tell my mom. She had enough problems of her own to deal with. And I do not want her embarrassing me about starting my period like she did when she took me shopping for my first training bra and had to tell the world.

And I do not want my sisters to know because they will tell everyone at school. Sometimes I hate my school. Well, most of the time, actually. And it's not that I hate *school,* because I love learning new things and making new friends, and to be honest, I'd rather be at school than at home because of the ugliness that goes on all the time. I just hate how people at school create so much drama, and most of the time, they are lies and rumors that only end up hurting others like when my sister told everyone that I sucked my thumb.

One day Michael Donahue told everybody that his dad was gonna fire Sister Body Parts 'cause he was on the school board and he didn't like her. Most of us were actually very excited until Sister Body Parts told Michael that he needed to report to the school office lavatory to get his mouth washed out with soap and water for lying.

She was fired the next day.

And Michael Donahue suddenly became my unofficial adviser.

CHAPTER FOURTEEN

It's all about Me

So here I am. The new me. The Riley Patton without the boy crush, obsession, whatever it was. I realized I don't need a boyfriend to be happy with myself. That was a big, "Ah-ha! Moment." Maybe I'm too young to have those ah-ha moments, but something big has changed with the way I feel and think right now. It really feels good to not have to have a boyfriend. I feel free to explore things just for me. And that's a rare deal entirely, especially as one of five kids.

It's never about me. What do *I* want? I wish I could answer that. I know that it's the end of the school year and summer's coming, and that means sun and fun, somewhere. Our church is trying to sign people up to serve a mission in another country somewhere doing something. I'm not sure, but I think I'm gonna see if I can go. I'm sure my parents will say yes because that will be one less kid to deal with this summer. But then again, my parents will have one less babysitter, too. I wish I could charge my parents. I'd be rich, and then I could travel anywhere in the world I want.

So now that I'm on this "it's all about me" campaign, I'm putting my Girl Scout embroidering badge to work. I embroidered the following on my favorite pillow: "I love me." I'm going to embroider, "I love me," on other things, too, so I can see it everywhere I look even though I know Kat is going to make an ugly comment just because she always thinks it's always about *her*, but guess what, Kat; it's not. Take that, Kat.

Kat is someone who has to have a 24/7 boyfriend. Maybe inside she's just jealous of me because she knows she's so insecure and I'm not because I'm a whole person just as I am. She's like a half a person and her boyfriends are the other halves. I read that in a teen magazine when I was waiting in the dentist office with my mom. She smiled when the dentist told her I don't have any cavities. I'm not sure why she was surprised since we can't eat candy during Lent and we never have the money for sweet stuff like desserts.

And my parents never buy soda 'cause it will rot our teeth. One time my brother Danny pestered my mom so bad to drink a Coke that she said, "Sure, but you are supposed to drink Coke really fast to get the best taste the fastest." So he stupidly followed my mom's advice and took one long, really big, fast gulp and nearly died. Well, he didn't *really* nearly die, but his eyes lit up like a football stadium at night, and they watered like a flood in spring, and the poor guy coughed and coughed until parts of his lungs shot out of his mouth like the worst scary movie scene ever. Well, maybe I'm exaggerating a bit. But it was so awesome! Danny doesn't drink Cokes anymore. Sometimes I think my mom really does know what she's doing. I gotta give her credit on that one.

If I kept score on the number of boyfriends I have had compared to the number Kat has had and still has, I'd be losing big time. But would I really be losing? Maybe Kat is the biggest loser. I just now envisioned Kat with a big black "L" tattooed on her forehead that would even show through on Ash Wednesday when the priest puts an ashen cross on our foreheads. I'll have to keep this vision top of mind, especially when she tries to make me feel like I'm less than she is.

But if I decided to have a boyfriend, I think I would want Michael Donahue, but I'm not sure if he wants a girlfriend right now. He seems to be real busy being the leader of the school. It's weird… when Michael speaks people listen, even the nuns. Why is that? I would love to have that kind of power. Maybe I'll ask Michael how he gets his power. I wonder if he asks God for it. "Dear God, please give me the power to say things that make people listen. Amen."

I don't think it's that easy, though. Maybe you have to be born with it. I know I was born with the skill to be a writer. Maybe I'll write speeches for Michael when he runs for president of the student council, and that way people will listen to me through him. Way cool. Awesome girl power. Go me!

If I'm to travel the world and write speeches for famous people like Michael Donahue and serve on missions, then I'm gonna need to learn a foreign language. I think I'll learn Spanish since I know a little bit now. I have friends in class who speak Spanish. The nuns don't like it when they speak Spanish in class because they don't know what the students are saying, except for Sister Dorez and Sister Salvador, who reply to them in Spanish which makes the other nuns mad – no, jealous I think. That is, if nuns get jealous. They're not supposed to get jealous because that's a sin, I think. I know a few words that the Spanish kids say and I know they make fun of the nuns, and I giggle and then cough so I don't get in trouble for laughing at the nuns because that's a sin, too, I think.

It's tough business trying to keep up with all the sins of the world. It seems like the nuns make up new ones every day. I kinda have learned that, at any given moment, I'm probably committing a horrific sin. I wonder if other people walk around like that. Just the thought makes me want to smile even bigger, smile like sunshine.

My mom walks around like a black cloud, and it makes me want to bring sunshine into her life. So that's why I do and say goofy things sometimes. I want to make my mom laugh and smile. I want to make my dad laugh and smile, too, so he'll stop drinking. They're both dehydrated 'cause they see the world as half-empty. Maybe if I serve on a mission, they will be happy and proud. Sometimes I struggle with focusing on me so the "all about me" is actually a challenge, which probably sounds a bit strange since most kids are self-centered by nature. Maybe I'm more selfish than I realize.

It's also tough business being a Catholic girl. I realize I can be mad, sad, bad, or glad.

So today, I choose to be glad. We'll see what the summer brings. I think for the next school year, I'm gonna "go fad" and bring some fashion sense to the stupid ugly uniforms we have to wear. I have so much to do; I don't have time for a boyfriend anymore.

About the Author

Amy Gallagher loves inspiring young minds as an English/Language Arts teacher for middle school and high school students. As the "Apple Lady," she wrote a healthcare column for local newspapers and enjoys presenting nutrition topics as a guest speaker at schools and businesses. As a journalist by education, Amy has been published internationally in healthcare and aviation magazines and had her first piece published at the age of ten in a major newspaper. She is also a "recovering Catholic school girl" and welcomes feedback from other recovering Catholics. As a proud mother of a beautiful son and two step sons, she lives in Fort Worth with her husband and their two "girls"... a toy poodle and a Jack Russell terrier.

To read more by Amy Gallagher, visit her website:

www.amycgal.com